An Irish Lullaby
a novel

Pamela Mary Brown

To those who have been subjected to sexual violence.

Prologue

Post-mortem photography

The trees were still and the smell of rotting pine needles filled the morning air. A soft haze shrouded the scene. Dull shafts of light struck smoky and solemn and spear-like through gaps in the trees. Everything seemed stationary…time…movement…sound…like a ghostly snapshot…and then having to walk into it…having to move forward and become part of the photograph…I began to shake and I don't know whether it was from cold or fear or lack of sleep…or shock…but that was it, it was over and I had found her…I tried to move forward but I couldn't…maybe I shouted…I know there was a sound, but I am not sure if it came from me.

Book I

Rathford, County Donegal
Present Day

Joe Doherty's body lies a moulding in the grave

I had returned for my father's funeral…not that I cared that the aul bastard had finally bit the dust. I just wanted to see his corpse go into the ground, spit on his grave. Anything that would help me finally leave behind all the obsessive compulsive thoughts about what I could do to him. Almost thirty years was far too long to carry that shit around.

I had returned for my… I deliberately chose a pew that was almost full to capacity.

'Sorry, sorry, excuse me, sorry,' I whispered politely and repeatedly as I pushed my way right to the very end, sitting myself down unruffled and upright, perched like Lady Macbeth in principal position ready for the second act.

Here is the church, and here is the steeple
Open the door and see all the people

My anonymity afforded me the luxury of a dramatic entrance and I had executed the manoeuvre skilfully, the objective being to wade in unperturbed, whilst at the same time, strategically disturbing the reverence. I had returned…I wanted to savour the hissing and muffled shuffling made by those who had to momentarily halt their prayers and alter their kneeling positions in order to accommodate my imposition. So that was that, easy as *Scrumdiddlyumptious* apple pie from a Fanny Cradock recipe book and I was once again among the rank and file of small town nowhere.

Home again, home again, jiggity jig.

I was confident that no-one would recognise me. I had made damn sure of that. An innovative choice of disguise meant I didn't look entirely out of place. I wasn't about to be crowned the prodigal daughter and the last thing I wanted was to have to explain my presence to anyone.

On a face non-recognition scale from one to ten, I would have given myself a good nine.

'Step forward please…state your name for the record…and then return to the line up.'

'No, no, no, thon's definitely not the Adele Doherty we knew, that wan's not from around these parts at all.'

DRAMATIS PERSONAE

ADELE DOHERTY, lethal daughter of the deceased.
JOSEPH DOHERTY, deceased, King of Cunts.
LAUREN DOHERTY, wife of the deceased, defiled-domestic-doormat mother, punch-bag slave and skivvy.
MARTIN, friend to Adele, Prince of Queens.

KAREN
NEILL
MARIE
JOSEPH   abandoned children of the deceased.
PATRICK
ELIZABETH

ANNIE, the town fool, Queen of Crazies.
PEARL, mother of the deceased, tough as old boots.
MONICA, mother-in-law of the deceased, Queen of Martyrs.

I straightened my spine confidently in order to improve my vantage point. Not one single solitary soul on the face of this earth knew that I would be here. Well, except for Martin…he had helped me with the subterfuge and had desperately wanted to come with me, but this was something I had to do alone.

'Are you sure you'll be alright?

'I'm grand now, Martin, honestly, don't be worrying yourself, I'm *fine!*'

I had lost count of the number of times I had to reassure him, but to be fair to Martin I did appreciate his sentiment and he had encouraged me to go home for the funeral. He said it would be

6

therapeutic, part of the 'letting go' process. Sometimes his intentions could be a tad airy fairy, but genuine nonetheless. I would give him a blow-by-blow account later anyhow. It would be something we could laugh about in safe haven bay over *some Fava beans and a nice Chianti.*

My eyes began to cautiously scan the church for my siblings but I would have been surprised to have seen them there. I knew Karen hadn't spoken to Daddy for years. Elizabeth and Marie might feel obligated to attend or maybe the boys would feel compelled by the aul genome of duty-bound. Honour thine ancestors kinda thing. After all, burying a parent wasn't something you got to do every day of the week. Well…unless it was Groundhog Day!

I've just stepped in to see you all, I'll only stay awhile, I want to see how you're getting on, I want to see you smile…

'Stop grappling for something that doesn't exist,' I told myself firmly. 'Your brothers and sisters wouldn't exactly stick the kettle on if you showed up on their doorstep… and remember your presence here is dependent on no-one recognising you, otherwise, *heavens to Murgatroyd*, you will have to *exit stage right*!'

I reminded myself that I was an impervious warrior, like Boudica or Joan of Arc or Emmeline Pankhurst or Grace O'Malley the tyrant pirate queen. I was among the enemy and was unfaltering. Imagine being privy to a room filled with people who had considered your life the main topic of parasitic gossip for years on end, boring little chit-chat lives with nothing better to do than chinwag incessantly about other people's heartbreak.

Technicolor painted wood carvings of the Via Crucis hung at regular intervals along the magnolia painted walls of the chapel. *Jesus comforts the women of Jerusalem* was my designated station, although Job's comforter seemed a more appropriate title for the scene.

On a hill far away stood an old rugged cross, the emblem of suffering and shame…

7

I cleared my throat rather more forcefully than I had intended and the natural acoustics of the building amplified the sound. The starkness of the noise made me realise that my mind had strayed.

'Fuck them.' I muttered under my breath, making sure that it sounded more like 'Amen' if I was overheard.

The defiant part of me was willing people to rise to the challenge and I would have loved to have goaded them,

'Bring it on you pack of red-neck hillbillies. Adele Doherty is all grown up!'

I could deal with their stares, the curious looks, the prying demeanours, the discerning judgements from locals who instinctively knew that their territory had been infiltrated. All must be known about the new arrival, the blow-in or the exile returned. No small town rested until the measure of such a person was intensely accessed and ruminated. I had been reared with that shit and they could all take a run and jump as far as I was concerned. At this particular point in the procedure my only regret was that I hadn't put my Daddy into the coffin myself. Death by natural causes was too good for the cunt.

I felt strangely taller, like a tourist in a model village and the past suddenly seemed to exist in some miniature form. After all I had only been a runt of a teenager the last time I'd set foot in the saintly Saint Mary's chapel. *Oh Mary we crown thee with blossoms today, Queen of the Angels and Queen of the May...!*

The plaster on the wall adjacent to my lookout position was exposed and revealed the crude red sinewed bricks. The outline of the defacement reminded me of the bloody town boundary, as if some artist had been given a commission to chip out the cartography. I could have drawn in the entire outpost. The chapel on the hill, the school under its shadow, the graveyard located beneath the playground, and the town snug and repressed below.

'The place has withered,' I told myself. 'It's still cold and dull and stinks of the same musty smell.' Well maybe a bit mustier or maybe I was no longer acclimatized to it.

The decrepitude of the chapel caused a seismic shift measuring about a '5' on my Richter magnitude scale. Everything had grown older but the vividness of my freeze frame memories hadn't aged at all. I realised that the faces of the people I recognized looked frailer, greyer but still feigned the same piety, genuflecting humbly as they manned their funeral poses ready for the ceremony.

'Coffin ahoy me hearties, all hands on deck.'

'This is bullshit,' I thought. 'Bullshit crap.' I would have loved to have shouted the words and hear them reverberate. The reverence was annoying me. I had psyched myself up for the war path and hadn't considered that people would look so bloody depressed.

I was overcome with an urge to just stand up and announce my presence…

'I'm over here, here I am.'

…or better still…puke into the baptismal font like some rabid animal. That would have woken them up, incited *mass* cardiac arrest. I could have taken a half a dozen of them out without laying a finger on them. There was nothing like a bit of foaming at the mouth to freak people out, and if Martin had been with me he would have insisted that I don a nightdress in order to commit such an act.

'All possessed women must be clad in a nightdress! Rule number one when conducting an exorcism on the female gender, the attire must be transparent!' I could hear Martin confidently espouse the appropriate guidelines, like he himself was a Vatican representative on the subject.

Nel nome del Padre, e del Figlio, e dello Spirito Santo. Amen.

I was beginning to wish he had come with me. Now I understood why he wanted to. He would be missing all the crazy fantasies we loved to create. They were such a good fun world to inhabit!

The chapel doors at the rear of the building slap-banged open and slap-banged closed again. All eyes turned to ogle who had entered. The town fool was now in on the act. I smiled mischievously on catching a glimpse of her and slunk a little into my seat.

'Annie has only one hat…Annie always wears a hat to weddings and funerals...one hat for all occasions…heeheehee…one hat suits all.'

People quickly averted their eyes from her attention as she waddled down the aisle. Nobody wanted her to bed down beside them. Annie chose a random pew and wriggled herself into it, she burped loudly, then nodded and grinned, toothless, to all in her trajectory.

'Better out than in…that's what Annie says…better out than in.'

I released a long sigh and realised that I wasn't the only person drawing the disapproving attention of my fellow congregants, so this time I said 'Amen' clearly, and settled down quickly. It was going to be a day for walking over graves alright. River dance had come to town and I would delay getting the tap shoes out just yet.

Deedle-dee, deedle-dee, bump-dee, deedle-dee.

The coffin had already been placed in the centre aisle and all looked ship shape for the proceedings. Head to the stern, feet to the bow.

'I name this vessel *The Hell Voyager*, God sink her to Hades and all who sail in her.'

The mood was appropriate and the ritual could be officiated according to *Canons 1176-1185* of the *1983 Code of Canon Law* for Catholic funerals. The Catholic Rule book wasn't one to be violated and they accepted all measure of sinners into their fold.

I nodded to myself, I was doing good, following my plan, just there for the funeral, in and out like a flash, better in than out, *heeheehee* but there is no such a thing as sanctuary in a town like Rathford… not even in a house of God…for then I saw him, 'Fuck Head' McGroarty.

DRAMATIS PERSONAE: SPECIAL-UGLY TREE- BRANCH
Sergeant PAUL, leading man evil bastard villain, Satan, Beelzebub, Son of Satan Snr, Keyser Söze, MCGROARTY F.H., Prince of the Pit, Hell Cat, Duke of Darkness, Devil of Damnation and the Festering Personification of Decomposing Rancidity and Pervert of Pure Petrifaction.

I felt as if my blood turned to sour milk, my arms and legs went limp. If someone had turned off my Newtonian gravity switch I would have blobbed my way to the ceiling like a bloated jellyfish. 'Fuck Head' didn't deserve to be alive. My eyes squinted defiantly and I ground my teeth malevolently.

'Pretty girl,' I could hear him saying. 'Pretty little girl, Joseph Doherty has certainly done well to breed a daughter like you.'

'Hell Fire Stoker McGroarty... Evil Club Honorary Member shouldn't have been able to enter a house of God! Surely that was in their bloody rule book!'

It would have been so easy to have killed McGroarty there and then, slit his throat or blown a hole in the back of his scabby head but I calmly reminded myself that my initial intent was to get out of Dodge City as quickly as possible but I also knew that he had to die so that I could close this never-ending-nagging book of my life.

I had returned for my father's funeral, not that I cared...I liked order; in all the crazy chaos it was the one thing that made me feel safe. I began to softly rock backwards and forwards, a little insecurity trait that I had acquired over the years. I wasn't at all prepared for McGroarty's presence to make me feel he had knifed me in the guts and smeared them all over my face. But I had deliberately ignored the thought of McGroarty so I could revel in the joy and relief that flooded over me when I heard of my Daddy's death.

Ding Dong! The Witch is dead. Which old Witch? The Wicked Witch! Ding Dong! The Wicked Witch is dead.

I hadn't let anything dampen my zest for *joie de vivre* on this my first visit home.

Then I remembered my *death wish list.* The memory triggering my hand into automatic reflex mode and as I reached inside my oversized handbag I couldn't believe that I hadn't packed a Smith and Wesson 29.44 Magnum that was as essential to any contents list as much as a humble tube of blood red lipstick.

After a brief second of careful rustling and homicidal musings I cautiously removed the piece of paper, the pages felt damp and the folds were threadbare. The list hadn't increased dramatically since my sudden exit from the town and I had only really thrown it in as an after-thought. Maybe there were a few people that had already kicked the bucket and could be removed from the short list... I don't know... the list just felt like it belonged here for most of the names on it were just my way of playfully making notes of the people that I intended to outlive. 'I'll see that aul bastard in his grave,' kinda stuff. But McGroarty, on the other hand, he was a whole different bloodbath and was in an exclusive category. 'O' for obliterate! Over the years I had taken the devising of his demise to a higher level and it had occupied me and frustrated me, as well as tested my inventiveness. I had contrived a couple of ideas in my head; Hitchcockian and Agatha Christie style, a Tarantinoesque slaying, death by a thousand cuts. I was definitely in favour of the extreme graphic violent horror-torture-type scenario. The chisel of time had given me the opportunity to develop several methods of annihilating that fucker.

Smiling, I recollected Martin's trust in Karma. Providence may actually be reliable, I thought. Martin had said it had a fortuitous way of presenting a situation that made payback possible. Maybe now it was granting me an opportunity, maybe now retribution was finally on my side. And sure there was no harm in giving Karma the occasional shove up the cause and kick-ass effect.

The organist abruptly woke, he spluttered and coughed heartily and without warning struck up a woeful sound, like a foghorn with acute sinusitis, everyone responded by standing up. The priest waltzed dignified onto the altar, he was dressed in a cheeky little black loose fitting Chasuble, embellished with intricate hand embroidery and matching stole. He swept his head to the side as if throwing back a fleece of invisible golden locks from his forehead.

daDadaDada, slight pause, lift the pedal*, daDadaDa daDadaDada…*the priests hands were outstretched as if carrying the soul of my Daddy. He offered it up to God almighty. I was certain that there wouldn't be a dwelling place prepared in the Lord's house for my brute of a father.

The priest's tone was forcibly solemn and he drew out the words like a drunken Gregorian chant at a midnight raid in the Vatican wine cellars.

Almighty God and Fath-er, it is our certain fa-ith that your So-n, who died on the cro-ss, was raised from the dea-d, the first fruits of all who have fallen asle-eeeeep.

My stomach somersaulted with nausea. Oh for God's sake…get bloody on with it. I thought impatiently. I have to attend the Texas Chainsaw Massacre!

Grant that through this mystery your servant Joseph Doherty, who has gone to his rest in Christ.

I said hurry up! Jesus Christ can priests not speed-read.

May share in the joy of his resurrection

Have you a reading age of five!

WeaskthisthroughourLordJesusChristyourSon,wholivesandre ignswithyouandtheHoly SpiritoneGod foreverandever. Amen.

'Amen, alleluia, praise the lord, ring the bells, rejoice. Rot in hell you evil bastard!'

Book II

Rathford, County Donegal
1987

Jesus was lost, Jesus was found

The sun had risen in Rathford like it had done every morning since the town had taken root. The fog had been slow to clear, but the birds sang, curtains opened and people emerged to embellish the fore and background; everything was usual. I couldn't understand why life hadn't stood still, another day had begun and Lauren was still missing.

There has to be a moment in everyone's life when everything stops. A defining moment that offers a clear and unequivocal view, a moment where an entire lifetime can be evaluated, where you have to swallow all that has gone before and know that if change is not embraced then something terrible will happen. I knew it was too late for my mother Lauren. I knew that she had had her moment of clarity and felt powerless. I knew something terrible had happened.

My bedraggled form stood unkempt and deflated before my Daddy. I could have stood unflinching for hours and he had unwittingly taught me the technique himself. Once, back in the scabby old days, when I was about eight or so, I had stood up during mass when I was supposed to kneel down. Sometimes it all got a bit confusing, all that upping and downing, and anyway he yanked me swiftly into the designated *on thy bended knees* position, while at the same time leaning rigidly into me and pretending like he was going to whisper something into my ear but instead he bit my earlobe and hissed threateningly between his teeth.

'You're always showing me up, doing stuff that will get you noticed, I'm going to teach you exactly where your place is, and nobody will notice you there!'

My ear was congested with the venomous saliva of this threat.

> **Craic** /cra ick/ *n*. before, during or aftermath
> storytelling, side-splitting fun and frivolity usually
> associated with copious alcohol intake; the ability to

relate *the craic* has earned the Irish the accolade of being the world's foremost storytellers. This word is also key to the survival of the Irish as a dispossessed race and subjugated nation, no matter how harrowing times became *the craic* could always be called upon to dissipate the inner and outer conflicts.

After the Mass was over Daddy huddled, as per usual, in the chapel grounds with a few of his cohorts. They smoked eagerly and jovially slapped each other on the shoulder. They threw back their heads while they laughed as if it was an after mass offering to the Lord above. He was in no hurry to leave the craic and he never once looked at me. I stood at the sidelines like a dejected substitute. My brothers and sisters waited in toe also, waiting for the big commander-in-chief man to make his move. Eventually he flicked his cigarette butt towards us as he headed towards the chapel gates. We automatically fell into line, shuffling forward on our anxious feet, hoping that our walk was the required pace as we set off to march the road home.

Daddy began to scowl at me once we were out of sight of the town. He poked and shoved me in the back to usher me forcibly along, like an irritated drover late for the fair. He was ensuring that the dramatic tension mounted appropriately.

'Don't you think for one minute that I have forgotten what I said to you, *little miss everyone in the whole damn world look at me!*' His voice was mocking and then he hissed again, 'I have somewhere in mind for you and nobody will notice you there…do you *hear* me!'

I could hear him alright. I mean I didn't think for one minute that he was suddenly concerned that he might have damaged my eardrum!

Stupidly I thought I was just going to get the usual battering and sent to bed to lick my wounds. The sort of punishment that we had grown accustomed to. Except this time he had decided on the *I shall break her psychologically* approach and as we turned into the laneway to our house Daddy grabbed me by the scruff of the neck and dragged me over the yard and crash bang landed me into the coalhouse.

'Stand you there,' he snarled. 'No, over there in the corner, a bit more to the right, that's it…freeze…I said freeze…and don't fucking move a muscle or I'll beat the living daylights outa you.'

He left me in the darkness, bolting the door from the daylight outside.

It became usual for me to frequent this dungeon and it was no luxurious 6 by 8 prison cell. It measured two baby steps from left to right and three from the door to the back wall. There was no window and the coal dust made me sneeze and clung to the hairs in my nostrils.

So when I was cast into solitary confinement I usually stood still in the corner and didn't shift…Daddy could have come back at any minute and you would have to be in the established position or he would know rightly that you had moved an inch or a centimetre or a millimetre. Lauren would sometimes come out at bedtime and bring me into the house. But Daddy usually dragged me out again and said I was only to come out when he said so. He was the boss man…yes sireee!

Eight years of standing motionless training developed into a honed skill that I would use to my advantage during many of his stupid interrogations. The aul theta waves had kicked in and my presence went into auto-pilot…my mind became mentally disengaged.

Mork calling Orsen. Come in, Orsen.

The gap between us was invisibly defined, as if a line had been drawn and I knew exactly at which distance from him I was required to stand. Like some sort of mathematical code written into the ether of the shortest distance between an abusive father and his demoralised teenage daughter. My arms flopped submissive by my side and my head was tilted slightly to the right. Daddy was eyeballing me.

'Look at me.' He kept saying while almost stabbing his right eye with his index finger.

I would have loved his finger to have slipped, to see him gouge out his own eye.

'Just a teeny bit higher and a bit more force,' I thought, 'now that would be a fine sight for sore eyes.'

'Look at me!' he repeated.

'Funny,' I thought to myself, 'he looks tired today.'

I was used to studying his face, observing every crease and crevice, every slight alteration in muscle tone.

'Don't you dare look away when I ask you a question,' he said fixedly. I hadn't looked away but Daddy needed to assert his dominance by repeatedly overstating whatever point he felt the need to hammer home.

If I had a hammer, I'd hammer in the morning, I'd hammer in the evening, all over this land…

'Look at me!' his voice rose.

This time I straightened my head, just to make him feel that he had somehow achieved something.

'Are you sure you don't know anything?' He delivered the sentence as if there was a full stop after each word.

I just shook my head blankly, that's what Lauren and I had agreed. Lauren had told me not to tell anyone what she had decided to do. I was not about to betray her request.

I continued to examine him, while he, in turn, scrutinised me. It was a stupid standoff, for neither of us had any reason to trust or confide in the other.

Daddy's knuckles paled and reddened as he opened and closed his fists.

'Mr Polished Pugilist,' I said mockingly in my head. Daddy was well adept at pushing people around especially when it involved teaching us *cretins* on the lower pecking order a lesson or two.

The disdain I felt for him tasted metallic on my tongue and then for some unknown crazy mental irrational yahoo gung-ho reason I had this gentle impulse to reach out my hand and touch him…to just brush his face softly and tell him to stop.

'There, there…it's all over…you can stop this now…you have finally got what you wanted all along!'

Whack for me daddy-o, whack for me daddy –o, whack for me day-o, there's whiskey in the jar-o…

Daddy was broad and muscular and his stomach was solid and his physique seemed impenetrable. He had a thick mat of dark wavy hair and there didn't seem to be any individual strands and even at forty-three he hadn't a grey hair on his head. His arms and his neck and face were weather-beaten and his dark eyes glinted spitefully, as if the pupil expanded over the iris until there was no detectable colour pigment.

'Did she say anything to you, anything at all that could help work out where the hell she is?'

Again I just shook my head.

Daddy was furious with my resolve.

'Lying little bitch,' I could hear him saying to himself. 'I'll break her if it's the last thing I do.'

But he would have to bide his time. He was well used to getting the upper hand but with Lauren missing the last thing he would want would be to lose support of the local community.

'Yippee kay-yay! The posse's here!' I could sense that there were now a lot of people in the room.

'Jesus,' I thought, 'half the bloody town is gathering to look for Lauren…the whole bloody thing is a farce…the whole stupid pretence that everyone suddenly gives a damn.'

Ah boys we'd be lost without ye, mozie on up, get off your horse and drink your milk!

I wanted to snort through my nose and it was itchy and not scratching it was becoming unbearable irritating.

'I don't know where Lauren is!' I suddenly blurted out the words while still managing to hold his stare. I couldn't be bothered with his game anymore.

'Lauren,' he sneered at me, 'Lauren…you know I don't allow you to call your Mammy that!' Daddy growled like a Neanderthal and raised his hand and I didn't flinch and instead of hitting me he placed it firmly on my shoulder.

I knew rightly that he despised the informal way that I referred to Lauren and I had deliberately riled him. Why did the world and his mother give a shit what I called her anyway? Maybe it had just been an easy sound for me to make when I had been a wee wain. Maybe la, la, la had been easier to say than ma, ma, ma, simple as that. But it wound people up to no end and they couldn't keep their busy-body noses to themselves.

> **Wain** /wee un/ *n.* a cross-community slang term for child. Probably derived from Ulster Scots (further etymological detail has been classified until Peace Funding is made available).

'That's a strange one now, never heard the likes of it before, I mean why in God's name can she not say the word Mammy! Sure every wain in the country can say the word Mammy! She's a bit touched in the head alright!'

That name never seemed appropriate and the word just felt thick and awkward on my tongue. Lauren never seemed to mind and anyway it was only an issue when some halfwit noticed.

> **Halfwit** /haf witt/ n. a mocking term combining both scorn and incredulity aimed at those deemed unfathomable amongst many of the more secluded villages of Ireland. The term is often used in response to an action viz. I was going to put the clutch back in that car this afternoon and you've done it for me and now look at it you *halfwit* it has five reverse

gears and only one forward. A *Cretin* is the superlative of *Halfwit*, although when in each other's company, certain difficulties and confusions arise when trying to tell them apart.

My grannies, Pearl and Monica, the dim and the dull witted and the thick as a plate of under-cooked poundies, didn't like it either; they thought I was just being a smart arse or something. It really seemed to irritate them more than most and I was glad because I didn't like them anyway, so they could bugger off!

'Stupid Adele,' Daddy said patronisingly, 'stupid wee girl, you're Mammy is missing…and we're all *wile* worried about her…and this is a very serious matter…do you understand?' Again he accentuated each syllable but this time like a sneering Headmaster wanting to mortify the school dunce before feigning exasperation and turning incredulous to his attentive audience,

'That wain's like an aul broken carburettor…you try to give her a good kick start and still all you get is an aul broken splutter.'

Some of the voices in the room guffawed in unison with him while he dug his finger nails discreetly into my shoulder, squeezing just enough to give me a taste of things to come if I didn't co-operate.

I didn't give two shits about humouring him and knew full well that Daddy was too self-indulgent to be anything other than ignorant.

'Lauren,' I said softly to myself, 'her name was Lauren.'

The use of the past tense caused an unexpected surge of panic to rush through every last inch of me and I must have flushed beetroot red and then the fear of him noticing made me feel even more panicked.

'Where are you Lauren…where are you?' but the more I said her name the less definitive it became and it was a sound that no longer had any physical meaning. I tried to picture her face; her face would give meaning to the name. I wanted to close my eyes, but I wouldn't dare. Not with the way he was studying me. If only I could close my eyes and find an image of her, I would be okay again.

I'll not leave thee, thou lone one, to pine on the stem, since the lovely are sleeping go sleep, thou, with them…

'Get out of my sight!' Daddy shrugged me slightly as he finally backed off. I bowed my head and walked backwards out of his vision, my body eventually stopping and resting against the wall. I lifted my head to look at those who had assembled, but the room was blurred and my eyes couldn't focus and I realised they had welled up.

'I regret to inform you…*sniff*…that there has been an incident…*sniff*…which requires…*sniff*…without delay and in an orderly manner…*sniff*…that we all make our way to the designated assembly point!'

I knew everyone was gawking questioningly at me and I couldn't bring them into focus and they were all misshapen…we were all standing in a house of distorting mirrors and all I wanted to do was scream and run outside but instead I dried my face as quietly as I could with my cardigan sleeve.

'Yes siree, no siree, three bags full of shit siree!'

I had temporarily bought some time and I began to fumble with the hem of my skirt nervously…rolling and unrolling it awkwardly…trying to bunch it into even folds, like a fan or something. I was hoping people would get bored and look away for they all thought I was some sort of handlin' anyway and I suppose hadn't given them any reason to think otherwise.

Handlin /han lin/ *n.* a bad situation (often involving individuals) exceeding your lowest expectations and suddenly getting worse. [see also banjax]

'Since the day and hour that that wan was born there hadn't been bloody peace on earth. Drive you to an early grave she would.'

I was personally responsible for every outbreak of war. The wrongs of the world were entirely on my shoulders and people were never backwards in coming forwards with the reminders.

'A tough wain to rear, you'll be a long time grey.'

They couldn't even wait until I was out of earshot to air their opinions.

'Aye she was always a clumsy and ugly wee wain. It took her ten months before she was able to sit up straight…and then she crawled around on her backside in the dirt 'til she was four years old…it was a miracle that she managed to learn to walk in time to start school.'

I remember a sense of relief from both of my grannies the day I started school. They had come to gratefully wave me off.

'God bless her and thank the Lord!' they had said in harmony. Having a child with a defect was a personal reflection. I mean people might think that you weren't right in the head yourself.

Little did any of them know or care that I had just been using my early years to cultivate other necessary skills, like a feral child, I suppose. As the first born I was the wain that would become the designated interrupter of the slings and arrows. The wain that would have to figure out how to manoeuvre within the dynamics of my parents brutal relationship. The wain that set the appropriate patterns of response for those that followed. The one that told the others when to be quiet, when to stay in our bedrooms and when it was alright to sneak out and play and when it was safe to go home again.

What can you do when you live in a shoe and a mouse goes poo on your face!

Then in an instant, in the blink of an unbeknownst eye, everything gets mixed up and confused like a fog that only ever shifts momentarily and gives you glimpses that don't really seem to tell the whole story, but are just there to goad you with things you should have done or said differently.

'Shall we do a boil wash today, add a little bleach for good measure, blanch all the life out of you! Hang you out to dry and start all over again!'

'You'll wash that blouse stupid!'

'Oh Lauren…where are you?'

A needle in a haystack

People were organising a search party. There was a religious solemnity in the air and it was strange because nobody seemed to think that Lauren could have been taken, that she had been abducted by aliens who wanted to perform some scientific experiments on her, some slimy evil lizard beings from a planet inhabited by reptilians! Or that maybe she had just gone away, simple as that. No, no, no, everyone knew, and the 'worst' had been accepted inwardly. It was just that no-one was going to be the first to say it out loud. There was no gain in honesty. The unspoken had to be placed in the middle of a circle so people could join hands and dance around it.

The farmer wants a wife, the farmer wants a wife, heho me daddy oh the farmer wants a wife!

The farmer already had a wife and you have no idea how *he ho me daddy oh* tramped her into the ground!

'Aye, a bit on the aul late side, revellers, if you ask me.'

I could only muster disdain for those who were steadily turning up on the scene.

'Spectators are advised to use the designated paths and not to distract the players, please follow the on-course instruction to ensure that events run smoothly and that you have the best available view of the action.'

My bottom lip was bitten raw and my nerves were wrecked and then there was McGroarty…but I couldn't think about that, not yet anyhow.

Pearl, my Daddy's mammy was crying.

'Ah, God love her, she looks worried now, well, who would have thought it? Who would have thought there were tears in the aul prune!' I snorted repugnant at Pearl's seeming distress.

Pearl stood at the scullery door of the house blowing her cigarette smoke outside. She was trying sternly to suck back her tears with every fierce drag. Her nicotine stained fingers standing out against the colour of her high blood pressure cheeks. I knew I was adding to her distress, my very presence and tight-lipped demeanour riled Pearl.

'Fuck off you aul' bitch.'

I would have loved to have scowled at her, tipped her over the edge. But of course I would never say anything like that to Pearl. There would be hell to pay, for there was always hell to pay.

'Jesus Christ,' I thought, 'Jesus Christ never woke up one morning to discover he was living in hell.'

Pearl kept giving me the odd look, trying to be tender, trying to make me believe that I could trust her.

'She's not fooling me, why would her scorn for Lauren suddenly disappear, just because Lauren had? I mean why would she suddenly give a damn?'

Pearl was a fierce red-headed woman, like some ancient war weathered warrior, she dressed in huge hand knit cotton jumpers that bubbled with blackberry stitch and could have provided shelter for an entire tribe. But Pearl wasn't warm, she was rigid and proud and she had disliked Lauren from the day and hour she had met her. I had seen many occasions over the years when Pearl undermined Lauren, mocked her and ignored her, like she was simple and didn't deserve to exist.

'Thon's a half wit,' Pearl would say. 'A screw loose somewhere, if you ask me.' She would add for good measure.

'Well nobody asked you, you aul cow, but you had to volunteer the information anyway, make her feel even worse than she already did.'

Until that morning I suppose I was used to the way Pearl had treated Lauren and it was never something I thought I could do anything about.

'Don't you fucking speak back to your granny!' Daddy would roar as he clipped his hand across the back of your head. Pearl liked it when he put his wains in their place.

'You need discipline with wains, otherwise they'll run you riot!' Pearl would make definitive statements as if she had been

26

crowned queen of how to rear wains. I didn't hold much stock in what she said, I mean look at the shit job she had done!

I never intentionally stepped out of line, and just took what was dished up as best I could. People were the way they were and I didn't feel like they would change. Change was never on any agenda, day to day involved being flung from pillar to post, whatever way people's mood blew, you just got on with it. The people that I knew were hard, tough as old boots. The scowls and bitterness were palpable.

Pearl wasn't exactly alone in the way she ridiculed Lauren, but as I watched her, with her mock sincerity and her pathetic anxiety, I knew I could have gained a standing count with one clean upper cut.

'Wham and down she goes!'

After all, I had had a top-notch trainer!

Some of the men were going to drag the river, but I knew she wouldn't be there. Lauren would never have risked being rescued or seen and she would have wanted me to have enough time to leave. I knew that Lauren would make sure that no-one would stop her. The river was too obvious. The thought of the river hurt my head. Lauren would never have made me go near water!

Johnny McCafferty was offering the services of his boat, the 'Rosy Day'. Johnny was a man who had done this type of thing before and he knew the river well. Johnny knew the tides and in his day he had seen the river swallowing plenty of souls. Fishermen who had made wrong judgements, accidental drowning—or suicides, if the truth be told—and Johnny was the man to call on when you needed to anticipate where the river might spit a body out.

'Aul Johnny the man himself! Oh, he was the boy alright!'

Johnny could easily organise the men, direct them, for they respected his opinion in matters like this. Johnny took no prisoners. He possessed leadership qualities and when he spoke he tapped his foot rhythmically, as if there was a pump beneath it, so that when he asserted command of a situation his chest inflated with pride.

Johnny's deep monotone voice hung in the air, hovering like a mantra and people answered when a reply seemed necessary, like the responses at mass. Saying anything at all under bad circumstances is always better than letting the silence speak.

'Ssshhh, did you hear the penny drop? No, we must talk boys, better to play the game boys, play the game! That way we all get a part of the action!'

There was about half a dozen men in total, men who held their heads down and peered from below their eyebrows with shrewd countryside humility. Men who had never spoke to Lauren, men who couldn't have picked her out in a photograph, a pathetic line up of broken people at a Garda Station.

'For we will not betray the flaws boys, we will not speak of the cracks.'

Óró 'Sé Do Bheatha Abhaile, Óró 'Sé Do Bheatha Abhaile, Óró 'Sé Do Bheatha Abhaile, Anois ar theacht an tsamhraidh!

My anger was becoming more and more difficult to hold back. I loathed the way they were all standing there, like bidders at a cattle mart. They all wanted to be of the part of the furore, part of the search, all wanted to give their tuppence worth, add to the debate, the anticipation, but most of all, they would have their jig later in the pubs or on the streets and have a hands-on contribution when people shook their heads in disbelief.

'It's a terrible pity, isn't it, so it is…tut-tut-tut…no, you never really know anybody nowadays do you…and all those poor little scraps of wains, that's who I feel the most sorry for.'

I didn't want their sorries, 'fuck their sorries, it was far too late for sorry. And besides, they had no bloody idea what sorry was!'

I circled the backyard a few times, holding back my disgust, listening to the solemn tones, the whispers, the voices trying to pre-empt Lauren's thoughts, deduce her whereabouts, all believing that they brought some kind of insight and if they could all pull their random pieces together, then they could somehow map out Lauren's movements. They were like greedy prospectors on the trail of fool's gold.

I quietly slipped my hand into my pocket and felt the money. I had never had any money in my possession before. It unnerved me and made me feel responsible for something that I didn't understand. Lauren had given it to me. I didn't want to think of it as a bribe. She believed that I would be well on the way to safety by now, but I had been too frightened, too much of a coward.

The great escape

I had gone into town to get the bus like Lauren had instructed me to do. I had felt compelled by a sense of urgency and walked swiftly. I was purposeful, following her orders that played like a song in my head…

Four roads to Glenamaddy, four roads that drift apart, four roads to Glenamaddy, and four dusty byways to my heart…

… but when I arrived at the makeshift bus shelter, I was stopped short in my tracks, nothing seemed to make sense anymore and it was as if a button had been pressed, and a vagueness replaced something that had been unambiguously perceptible. How could clarity just disappear? I mean I knew I must get on the bus, but all of a sudden I couldn't understand why.

I loitered, bewildered and I'm not sure for how long and then there was a handful of people queuing in the main street and we all seemed to have the same intent but I didn't want to be part of them. I felt repulsed and their faces were taut and they frightened me and seemed moulded into a mood that they didn't know how to escape from. I began to rub my forehead repeatedly, trying to encourage my thoughts to return. How could you know something one minute and it could be completely gone the next?

The local Swilly bus service travelled into Letterkennedy, twice a day. There was an early morning bus about 8am and then another one around 1pm. You could never set your watch by them for nothing but the mizzle and the rain were reliable in this god-forsaken place!

But I somehow knew that if I got out of Rathford and into Letterkennedy then I would be more anonymous. I would be able to find the coach that Lauren had directed me to get on without feeling like I was being watched, but I had never got on a bus on my own before. People would just know I had gotten on to that bus, for looking over the shoulder was second nature, whether something was out of place or not.

I was finding it hard to stay focused. I wanted a hand to grab mine, a great big strong giant of a God almighty hand to come out of the clouds and pull me upwards out of the fog.

'What are you bloody looking at!'

I wanted to scream, tell people that they had no right to look at me.

The priest's housekeeper, Miss Noble, arrived on the scene. She was haughty and terse and held herself stiff like her backbone was made from the shaft of a brush. She began to scrutinize me, her eyes huge and round. Miss Noble had a way of leering down the spine of her nose in order to get a better view of her subject from above, occasionally she would have to tilt her head slightly in order to achieve this successfully, but she was tall and her height gave her a good overview. On her arm she carried a willow basket, woven into a neat square. Her elbow locked firmly against the handle so that the basket never seemed to budge. I was never tall enough to see what was inside it, but it seemed important.

Miss Noble prided herself on her reputation for wearing a good coat, summer and winter, come rain or high heaven or 30 bloody degrees scorching sun. Miss Noble never showed any flesh from the neck down, even modesty would have felt ashamed in her company. The only parts of her you ever saw were her pious face and her hair, crowning her head, hat-like, in large motionless waves, not even the wind could alter it.

I suddenly caught my breath and gave a long sigh of relief. Miss Noble wouldn't bid me the time of day let alone ask me anything about where I was going. I knew that I was beneath her, undeserving of her conversation, unless that is she wanted to give out about something. Remind the scum children that being second in command to a parish priest decreed respect. We would be the vermin left on the sinking ship while Miss Noble would direct the lifeboat and dissolved glowing into the morning sun! The choirs of angels gloriously parting the clouds and singing alleluia!

'Alle–bloody–luia you stuck up bitch!'

31

I stood there dejected, looking into the river, pretending to be uninterested or carefree or something that didn't involve talking to anyone. But I was as paranoid as hell and felt as if they could read my plans.

'Adele Doherty, foiled escape from Alcatraz, stopped in her tracks and put right back in her low-life place by Miss Noble and her willow basket! Contents undamaged!'

I sneakily continued to give the odd glance at the others in the queue; I wondered was anybody else planning an escape as well? Maybe we could all join forces, set up a task force and organize a special bus for escapees. A chartered bus that arrived stealthily in the dead of night and in the morning you were just gone! Vanished, disappeared, no smoke effects necessary!

'This is it boys, tonight we're going over the top....'

But then I couldn't think of anyone who would want to get on a runaway bus with me, people seemed to be contented with their lot and my family seemed to be the only one *busted flat* in sad old miseryville.

The rasping old bus came spluttering down the bray. I closed my eyes disappointed. The bus was late as usual, but not late enough to have given me enough time to gather up the courage that I needed. It sounded more like a steam train as it pulled into the side of the road and it hissed and seemed to object, spitting before it came to a halt. It stank of coagulated diesel clots and *four country roads* and it looked misshapen, dipping in the middle like an exhausted old bed-frame, the wheels looked like they would buckle out from under it at any moment.

I didn't get on it. I couldn't. And when the driver called out to me.

'Hey there girl, are you getting on or not?'

'No, I'm just waiting here on a phone call,' I replied.

It was too much information, I knew that instinctively and a simple shake of the head would have been sufficient so I looked away as soon as I spoke. I didn't want to know who had heard me or who was making assumptions with their beady eyes. I didn't want to be worrying about gossips on top of everything else.

'Would you believe it now! 'tis true, I'm telling ya, it was the Doherty girl for sure…for I saw it with me own eyes.'

Now my answer annoyed me and I knew it was a silly one, but it was plausible. There was only one phone box in the town and it was a popular meeting point. So many stories had been exchanged in its shadow and sometimes when the phone box was full of money it would give out free calls and then the queue would stretch along the main street, people would be phoning their families all over the world, thousands of long lost relatives adrift in Australia or some other ballad singing corner of the globe that they hadn't spoken to for maybe ten years or more.

'Oh the memories and tears that those in far, far away land could evoke! Twould fetch a bucket of tears from the eye of a newt! Hand on heart for languid effect!'

We should have a national day of mourning for the emigrants, I could send a formal proposal to the government, but then…there might be some of us that nobody would want to mourn.

I hesitantly decided to walk home again. It wasn't an easy decision for me to make and I was maudlin and confused. I just wanted to see Lauren one more time, that's all I wanted, just one more time.

'Eeny, meeny, miny, moe, Adele Doherty has nowhere to go!'

Choice paralysed me, because choice was never about what you wanted for yourself, the final decision had to fit in with so many other peoples plans, you could cause world war 666 without realising. So I stood frozen like a contagious myxomatosis rabbit, lamped in no man's land, unable to move, unable to speak, unable to stand up to some unwritten code that everyone tipped their hats to, some foolish way of life that made sure that you never rose above your station.

'That one thinks she's better than the rest of us…I mean who the hell does she think she is…a proper little know it all, a good slap would sort that attitude out, I mean we all know where she came from, huh, huh, huh.'

'Are you choking there missus!'

The town suddenly seemed oblivious to me but I kept my head down just in case and I hypnotically watched my feet as I walked.

When on the road to sweet Athy, A stick in the hand, A drop in the eye, A doleful damsel I heard cry, Johnny I hardly knew ya!

I headed onto the back road. There was a side lane at the post office that slipped you out of the town, dipping suddenly like a slide in a playground.

'Wheee…*hurroo, hurroo* and off you go now!'

The road home was over-shadowed by stern conifer trees…Sitka Spruce and Douglas Fir and Larch compacted tightly together. There was a narrow ditch on either side of the road and some of the roots had managed to burrow and crawl across it and spread their tentacles determined to push upwards beneath the tarmac. It made you feel that the road was alive and you had to watch your footing at all times because you could easily trip.

Our family home was the first house that you would encounter while *roaming in the gloaming*. The design was typical of the houses built by the Donegal County Council in the early 1900's. It was a two up, two down cottage. The image of an Irish cottage in most people's minds tends to be that of a one-storey dwelling with a thatched roof, pretty painted shutters and white washed walls. Some *home-sweet-home, Romantic Ireland,* little Longhouse that has survived the famine and is now a perfect image of aul picture postcard Ireland! But they're tombstones; those thatched cottages make me want to cry.

Our house was called 'the cottage' nonetheless and it made it seem romantic or something, but it was just a sad, dull, wee house with four miserable walls that precariously held our fractured lives together.

An extension had been added to the house in the 1950's while my great grandparents lived there. They had added on a bathroom, a kitchen, a scullery and they gave the house a backdoor. The extension stuck out in an L-shape, like an awkward thumb. It had a flat felt roof and looked like it was a cheap afterthought, a bit that had been wedged on, like a way to use up left over *Márla*. The outside toilet was eventually turned into a coalhouse, but as my great granda had grown older and his memory was going he used to still go out in the night and pee on the coal. Pearl said it was wrong to laugh because the coal still had to be burned and somebody had to go out and get it and that was usually her. So we only laughed when Pearl wasn't there. The coalhouse would become my prison cell.

The two bedrooms upstairs were occupied by us wains and the rooms were appropriately named, 'the boy's room' and 'the girl's room.' They were small and pokey and the ceilings sloped with the roof of the house so you were constantly stooping at different gradients as you manoeuvred around the bedroom, like the Grand Old Duke of York.

And when you were up you were up and when you where down you were down and when you were only half way up they were neither up nor down!

Lauren and my Daddy had a bedroom downstairs. We never dared go into it. The house always seemed to be in darkness and it had been built on a dip in the road and the setting was pokey anyway, so there wasn't that much hope of light getting in.

The house was hunched beside a little humpback bridge about half a mile from Rathford's main street and my family's feet had plodded the route so many times that we all said that we could have 'walked it blindfolded'.

At one time I would have considered taking up the challenge but it wasn't something I gave two damns about anymore.

No mammy's kisses or no daddy's smiles, nobody wants me, I'm nobody's child

I was well aware that Daddy would be at home when I got back and he would be wondering where Lauren was, but not in any caring way, that was for sure. He would probably be thinking that she'd gone wandering and had just lost track of the time, even though Lauren never went wandering. He would be annoyed with Lauren no matter what he thought for he was always annoyed with her.

I had a sensation of dread in my stomach, like I had eaten something rancid in a ravenous fit of starvation and it was making me even sicker. I pictured myself as a deranged carnivore from some psychotic Stone Age settlement, gnawing on some aul putrid bone.

My mouth was dry and my lips felt hacked and why the hell was I heading back? I mustn't have two brain cells to rub together. He was going to bloody kill me when he found out what I had done and it certainly wasn't the first time I had wished that he would just kill me and get it over and done with.

'Go on, kill me if you want, scumbag! One clean swipe and knock the life clean out of me.'

I just didn't know what else to do and the unfamiliar may have been frightening and even though the familiar was probably more frightening, at least I thought I could deal with it.

I slunk slowly along the road, trying to melt into the shadows, wishing that my life belonged to somebody else and that my Daddy had drowned in a tragic fishing accident years ago. Then everyone could have cried and pretended that they missed him, but deep down we would be glad that he was gone, hoping that he had struggled and fought and suffered before he swallowed his last breath.

I didn't feel the need to hurry. I would wait until the others had come home from school, safety in numbers, not that it had been much good in the past, but today of all days I really didn't want to be on my own with him.

My hands were cold and as I rubbed them together they hurt and I noticed that the palms were raw. I clenched them closed quickly. I wouldn't think about that. There were some things that could stay in the fog.

The wind was bitter, for it had been a mild winter and the early days of spring were chilled with the biting cold, a few little frozen snowdrops huddled in clumps on the roadside. People always say that we pay in spring for a mild winter, 'the weather is nobody's friend, no indeed it's not...not unless you live in Spain or Italy or somewhere! Oh dear God, why could people not stop talking about the bloody weather!'

I sat down along the edge of the roadside and hunched myself up on the ditch. I needed a bit more time to pass. I tried to picture Lauren's face. I desperately wanted to see her. If I could see her one more time then I would remember what it was that she had said. I thought I would have a go at saying a prayer.

'Hail Mary full of grace, get me the fuck out of this place,' I wanted something to erase the pain in my head.

'I have to pull myself together, Jesus Christ, Jesus Christ, why do so many people call your name when you never answer!'

I'm not sure at what point he arrived, maybe he had been watching me for awhile. Maybe he had followed me from the town. But those facts don't really matter I suppose and they just add to the quagmire of useless detail, confusing even more the stuff that can't be undone.

I just abruptly felt his shadow behind me and it moved forward quietly until it engulfed me and I was completely swallowed by it. The hairs on my neck and arms stood on end. I felt instantly threatened, like when you know you are in the wrong place at the wrong time but it is already too late to do anything about it.

'What are you doing sitting here at this time of the day? All on your own are you?' His question was snide and rhetorical and he knew rightly that I was alone and he spoke with ease as I turned uneasy to look at him. He was holding a shotgun comfortably in his hand.

'I'm waiting on the others,' I said. 'School will be over now and they will be on their way home and I thought I would come out and meet them.' I tried to sound casual.

'Have you taken the day off? You know that if you are skipping school then it is my duty to make sure it doesn't happen again. I have a duty of responsibility.' His uniform buttons gleamed in the frosty sun.

'Nay, I was sick this morning, but I thought the fresh air would do me good.'

'Is your Daddy at home yet? I was speaking to him last night, he wouldn't be happy if he knew you were skipping school.' McGroarty had moved around me and was now in full view, standing directly in front of me.

'I'm not skipping school,' I said defensively as I stood up and tried to brush the pine needles from my clothes.

'You are a pretty little thing,' he rubbed his knuckles against my cheek making me take an awkward step backwards. I winced slightly as my foot lodged into an unanticipated hole in the ground. I carefully twisted and removed it while cautiously taking another step back, deliberately trying to steady my stance.

I didn't need to be told that being on my own with McGroarty was a bad idea.

'Your Daddy was talking about you last night.' He moved forward and this time he took my chin firmly in his hand and directed it upwards towards his face. My head was racing, why would Daddy talk to anyone about me? Daddy didn't give a shit about me.

'Joseph was saying what a pretty little thing you had become, a pretty little thing indeed.'

I twisted my face out of his grip and tried to move sideways. I wanted to run. I wanted to break into a sprint and keep running until I was at the ends of the earth.

'I have something I want to show you!' McGroarty said as he tightly gripped my upper arm. 'I will keep your secret and give you a special secret to keep all to yourself…then we'll be even.'

'I need to go home,' I said trying to shrug him off. 'I need to get back, Lauren wanted me to help make the dinner…so I better get going.'

'All in good time,' he said. 'All in good time. Now, are you going to come with me, like I asked, or do I have to use this?' He lifted the shotgun persuasively into the air.

'It's easy to mistake a young girl all alone out here for a wild animal…and I'm out here investigating a report about a wild animal. I can easily verify that back at the station.'

McGroarty as he rested the shotgun over his shoulder looked like a soldier about to go on active duty.

He held me firmly by the upper arm. I tried to drag my feet as he pulled me a few steps into the forest and it took very little effort on his part. McGroarty calmly set the shotgun down at our feet, the handle pointing towards us.

'Now, I won't be needing that,' he said as he pushed me roughly up against the coarse bark of a tree.

'So, what have we got here?'

I raised my hand defiantly and made a swing at him…exerting as much force as I possibly could. But he just grabbed my hand like he had the ability to freeze time and I couldn't move it in any direction. Then he pushed it down by my side as he leaned his weight forward and firmly placed one arm across my chest, pinning me motionless. I felt tiny.

The tree was jagged against my back and I tried to wriggly fiercely but he kept pushing me harder and harder into it. My heart and soul and every last inch of my innocent being knew that this was going to be the most terrible thing that could happen to my life.

McGroarty slowly began pulling my skirt up like he could dictate the ticking of the seconds that passed with the movement of his hands. His crude touch felt horrible on my skin and I closed my eyes as tight as I possibly could and turned my head to the side. His breath was foul and smelt of stale alcohol. He put his cold hand inside my pants and I didn't move…I couldn't move. I wanted to cry for Lauren, but I knew it was too late. I knew there was nobody in the whole world that could help me.

I tried to pray again, 'Hail Mary full of grace the lord is with thee…' I tried to pray and then I couldn't see Lauren and all I could feel was McGroarty's breath and I couldn't remember the rest of the prayer. I couldn't remember the words to a prayer that was mumbled day in and day out and resonated it's vibration to cover up the unclean thoughts of our contemptible souls. Prayer was supposed to save you. Prayer was suppose to hide all your fears in the shadows.

'Oh dear Jesus, maybe I'm being punished for taking your name in vain. I'm sorry God, I'm *wile* sorry for saying all the bad things I ever said about you!'

But there was nothing I could do, there was nothing I could say that would make him stop and there was no prayer that could make him disappear. I could only wait until he was finished. Just stand there and let him do what he was doing. I didn't want to think about what he was doing. Daddy's beatings were easier to imagine.

'Come over here you little piece of shit…I'm gonna teach you a lesson or two that you won't forget in a hurry!'

McGroarty was mumbling and grunting and I was trying to block him out of my head. His frame was heavy and he kept pushing it firmly into me. I just wanted the fog to come, if the fog came again, I could curl into it and I wouldn't feel anything either.

Then a song came into my head, a stupid corny song and I reached out and grabbed it like it was a pathetic wish shaken from a dandelion clock.

As I was slowly passing an orphan's home one day, I stopped there for a moment, just to watch the children play, It is so much easier to sing lonely songs than to deal with what was going on. *Alone a boy was standing, and when I asked him why, He turned with eyes that could not see, and he began to cry.* Somebody else's

40

pain is easier; somebody else's sad story will console you. There is always someone far worse off and we should take comfort in that!

Between my legs was too small for him and I felt like he was going to split me open. I must have tried to scream out the pain because he moved his arm and put his hand over my mouth and then I wished I would stop breathing. The only way to end this was to stop breathing, Lauren was right; she should have taken me with her.

People come for children and take them for their own, But they all seem to pass me by, and I am left alone, cry for what isn't real *ssshhh* you will feel better soon, *I'm nobody's child, nobody's child, I'm like a flower, just growing wild,* oh god help me, please somebody help me, what was I supposed to do? *No mammy's kisses and no daddy's smile...* The song overwhelmed me for a while and I looped its sombre melody in my head, it gave me more consolation than prayer ever could and it felt more honest.

And then a switch was pressed somewhere and it stopped and I slumped to the ground and it was all over. McGroarty had taken a step back. He was zipping up his trousers. He grinned gratified.

'Get up outa there now and run along home.' He didn't take his eyes of me as I tried to stand up.

'Adele,' he said, his voice had softened. 'You're a pretty little thing aren't you? Did you enjoy that wee Adele?'

I looked away from him and hung my stupid head!

'Joseph has certainly done well! Pretty little girl...not to worry now, we will do this again, and remember this is our secret, now we are even!' McGroarty lifted the shotgun as he spoke.

I suddenly realised that I was crying and the snotters where tripping down my nose and I kept wiping them onto my sleeve. I made a useless effort to stand up but my legs were weak and everything kept revolving. I couldn't make it stand still. McGroarty reached for me by the arm and pulled me forward onto my feet.

'It hurts the first time, sure every wee girl knows that...it was your first time...wasn't it...now don't be going and upsetting yourself.' He said this almost as if to console me and then he smiled, 'but you will enjoy it as much as me the next time. Go on, scoot, away home with you now.'

He shoed me like I was a fly.

Book III

Rathford, County Donegal
Present Day

Of all the Graveyards in all the towns in all the world

I started to feel claustrophobic. The air in the chapel suddenly felt thick and unbreathable and the smell of incense chokingly wafted and irritated my nostrils.

'Oh dear Jesus,' I thought, 'we're losing cabin pressure…it looks like we're going down. Please secure your own oxygen mask first before assisting others.'

I was about to take a full scale panic attack. I took a huge gulp of air and held my breath.

'Is there a first aider on board? Some Jane Doe has just collapsed and is in immediate need of resuscitation? But remember folks, thou shalt not exchange bodily fluids in a house of God!'

I placed my hand shakily against the chapel wall and it was cold and thick with the years of paint upon paint and I was trying to will myself to disappear into the dank soupiness and emerge unscathed on the other side of the wall.

'Why, oh why had I decided to trap myself…position myself in a place that made it difficult, if not completely impossible to get out of again. I hadn't thought…I hadn't envisaged such a big turn out to the funeral. But then how could I have forgotten what a popular man Daddy had been.'

We worship thee, we give thee thanks, we praise thee for thy glory!

I felt woozy and all in the chapel was in a bit of a tail spin. 'Wow you've got to pull yourself together old chap...gung-ho and all that poppy cock!'

Oh Lord, Heavenly King, God the Father Almighty…!

Why had I naively thought that this was some sort of a game? I had let my guard down. I should have prepared myself for seeing McGroarty. I should have let Martin come with me. I needed to get out of this God forsaken chapel.

I was well accustomed to checking my exit points. Why had this slipped my mind? It was common practice for me to ensure that I knew every escape route from any enclosed space.

'We would now like to tell you about some important safety features on board this aircraft, the boeing 747. Please watch our demo carefully and read your safety booklets before takeoff. There are 12 exits aboard this plane, 2 towards the front, 2 before the wings, 2 over the wings, 2 behind the wings, 2 at the rear of the aircraft and 2 in the centre of the upper deck.'

I reprimanded myself for being so remiss. What the hell had I been thinking?

'Okay,' I said to myself, 'you can do this, you can get out of this shit hole, the next time everyone stands…just start pushing yourself out of the pew…easy peasy lemon squeezy.'

I knew it was going to be difficult to leave discreetly. But then I said reassuringly to myself, 'what the hell are you worried about? Just look at what your Daddy and McGroarty have done, no-one ever turfed them out of anywhere on their ear! Calm yourself down for the love of mother Mary and on the count of three...! One, two…'

As if they could read my thoughts people began to stand, the noise of which started like a jet engine, bashful at first and rumbling nervously for awhile before take off until all were on their feet. I rose to the opportunity, standing swiftly and lifting my overhead baggage and using it to cover my flustered face.

The attempted escape had been instigated and the people in the communal pew were visibly dismayed when they yet again realised that they had to lean back in order to accommodate my bulkiness. Peoples knees were not designed to bend the direction in which I required them to but they had no choice and flexed awkwardly as I shoved past.

I moved determinedly but was unable to do so as quietly as I had hoped. A small clatter resounded as I caught my foot on the kneeler and it banged to the floor and I scraped my ankle and dust billowed gleefully but I continued to propel myself forward and finally regained my balance as I stepped onto the isle.

A plethora of faces turned to look at me, backs of heads suddenly had eyes and noses and mouths and other appropriate facial features, well maybe some features were inappropriate, but I had no time to think of corresponding images.

I was in the midst of genuflecting humbly and had a half bended knee when I realised that I didn't feel like observing the ritual…I stood again quickly, turned swiftly and waddled my way to the main double arched doors at the back of the chapel. The people standing beneath the alcove had to part to let me through. The continuation of the disturbance made the priest make an unprecedented and obvious pause, but I didn't look around to check his expression. I muttered some words of thanks to those who had accommodated my exodus and was outside before I exhaled.

'Bastard,' I said to the silent grotto, 'dirty rotten stinking Fuck Head bastard!' The statues didn't alter their expression.

'Oh dear Jesus, God and his mother help me!'

I desperately swallowed the damp April air and I was bowed over double and I didn't know if I could straighten myself up and still be able to hold everything inside.

'I'm in the loonie bin. I've willingly surrendered myself to this nuthouseville madness!'

> **Loonie bin** /*loon knee binn*/ n. a holiday destination
> for **halfwits** and **cretins**, especially a place unconcerned with
> mental health care yet provides free medication and EST on
> or without request. Can also be a convenient location to take
> visitors from England after plying them with beer and
> claiming 'they just started talking with an English accent can
> we book them in for a week?'

Drop your weapons and come out with your hands in the air!

I stood upright and turned. I felt as if someone had followed me from the chapel. I was relieved to discover that I was alone, just myself and the holy family in the hallows of the chapel grounds!

A brisk jaunt was the order of the day and it would do me the world of good, cheer me up and clear the head, so to speak. I had no thought for where I was going but was unable to strut as confidently as I had anticipated. Every step I took felt like there was melting tar beneath my shoes.

Huston, Tranquillity base here. The Eagle has landed.

I lumbered around the building towards the back of the chapel and upon turning the corner the graveyard immediately caught my eye. It sloped downwards towards the town and from my vantage point I could see a freshly dug grave. I stopped and smiled knowingly, feeling slightly revived and indulgent.

'That one is ready and waiting just for you, Mr Joseph Doherty! And no better place for you to be heading. God look to the little wormy beasties that try to feast on your poisonous corpse!'

Hear ye, hear ye, hear ye…From this vile world with vilest worms to dwell.

I walked a few feet further and then without thinking I sat down on a small stile that offered an opening in the grey wall that defined the enclosure of the graveyard. I hunkered my knees up comfortingly under my chin and wrapped my arms tightly around them to keep them in place.

I thought I might cry and I squeezed my eyes shut and gave it a go but I couldn't and there wasn't one drop of remorse in me for anyone of those savages. I couldn't even feel sorry for myself and the time for tears was long passed.

'This isn't my life and I don't belong here…I never belonged here.' Daddy was long dead in my mind. I had killed him a hundred times over and I had killed him every time I had a memory of him and maybe a good mental killing spree would sort them all out and I was pretty razor sharp at the visualisation.

47

'Oh Martin, queerest one, why did I not listen to thee, I wish that you where here with me right now! How do you solve a problem like Adele? You must leave the convent; become a governess to a dashing captain's brat children.. *do re me fa so la te do*…the graveyard is alive with the sound of…oh that's right…no it's not…they're all dead!'

'But I'm still alive and in one piece!' I was nodding to myself and must have looked like a dunking duck with the erratic rocking back and forth.

'All is not lost! And an aul pat on the back wouldn't go amiss. I've shown considerable constraint given the circumstances. I mean I didn't rip open the coffin lid with my teeth, jump in and stab the Daddy bastard dearest, much as I would have taken great delight in doing so.'

'No', I thought, 'stop berating yourself…you are doing pretty damn fine all things considered.'

'Anyhow, Martin I deeply regret talking you out of coming with me. And I know you will never say…*na na nanana I told you so*…but I do wish you were here with me for I don't like the feeling of being all alone in the world…like Lauren must have felt.'

I stood up again and stretched. The wads of padding that were layered around my body were helping to keep me warm but I decided to keep on the move.

'There is a nip in the air today by God!'

'And that was the latest golden nugget weather update…stand by for another instalment in sixty seconds or less.'

I began to walk carefully among the graves, manoeuvring so that I didn't step on any. It was tempting given the day that was in it, but it was unlucky to walk on a grave for any amount of disaster could befall.

'Tut-tut, I told her to stay off the graves…but she wouldn't listen and now look at the mess she has caused, never had an ounce of respect that one!'

I wasn't sure if I moved consciously or sub-consciously. I registered some of the names on the Headstones. O'Donnell. Sheridan. McGinty. Brown. Names I remembered from school or those of neighbours. Before I knew it I was standing in front of a plot with a simple granite headstone and a bog standard, bog basic minimum required information-only-inscription;

Lauren Doherty (nee Peoples)
Born 1954 – Died 1987
RIP

The white lettering was weathered a bit but the grave didn't look unkempt. The grass had been recently mowed, but there were no flowers on it, no plastic icons or token soap-stone angel statutes, nothing to show that a recent visitor had had sat with their sadness for awhile. The grave just seemed ordinary. Just like any grave.

'Of all the graveyards, in all the towns, in all the world...' This was it and I knelt down, for it seemed appropriate and I had never knelt at my mother's grave before. My head stooped humbly and my hands closed into the prayer position and I rested them on my stomach. I suppose some part of my demeanour was paying a mark of respect to her place of burial but the act was nothing more than one of forged emulation...because I knew that the bit of her that was in there was not the important part of her that I carried with me. It's just a stupid hole in the ground that we will all end up in one day and there isn't a damn thing anyone of us can do about it.

The dates on the headstone made me calculate how old Lauren would have been if she had still been alive and then I shook my head in disbelief for it was weird to think that I was now older than her...that I had actually managed to survive on this planet for longer then she had... imagine being older than your own mother.

The thought depressed me and I sat forlorn and wearily turned my head to look at the town. The sun was breaking through the puff ball clouds and the smell of the earth and the grass and the air prompted so many reminders. I twisted my body around and squatted down on the grass verge and tried to assimilate to the changes. The place had modernised considerably but I wasn't the least bit interested and it kept reverting back to the way it had been in my memory. The people would have needed to be exterminated, the place fumigated and then resettled in order for me to have felt that anything could have changed. Genocide in small town Ireland. So many invaders had tried and failed.

Proudly the note of the trumpet is sounding, Loudly the warcries arise on the gale, Fleetly the steed by Lough Swilly is bounding, Onward for Erin! O'Donnell abu!

Let us all march and wave our bloodied banners gleefully in the air!

An Bhaile Bheag agus an Aonach Culchie Mhóira

'Welcome ladies and gentlemen to Adele Doherty's flashback tours incorporated, limited by small mindedness and indoctrinated for good measure. You may notice a somewhat bitterness to my tone, but resentment is quintessential and emblematic of the location, so attune your ears accordingly and quit your bloody whining! If you look straight ahead and keep your opinions to yourself we shall begin!

Our virtual tour takes place in the year of our good and almighty Lord, nineteen hundred and eighty seven. The world is on the verge of changing technologically, a skin shedding evolution is about to begin, a property boom is getting ready to gobble up the horizon. But it will be a few years yet before it desecrates our dear little Rathford where gossip chatters like knitting needles contracted to turn out Aran jumpers for the Yanks.

Notice ladies and gentlemen how the river Harrison slices the town perfectly in half and it is certainly the main focal point of the setting. The brow-beaten, tenacious fishermen are a regular feature along the river banks and an IQ test of the fishermen would undoubtedly reveal that no salmon of knowledge was ever caught here.

There's no earthly way of knowing, which direction we are going, There's no knowing where we're rowing, Or which way the river's flowing.

If you look slightly to your right you will see an old boat yard rusting beside some aging stone buildings and a quaint quay. A little bit of heaven on earth, ladies and gentlemen, this is Ireland after all and our beautiful, beautiful Rathford is nestled snug in a little valley, cradled by a patchwork blanket of rolling fertile hills.

Is it raining, is it snowing, Is a hurricane a–blowing,

Visitors are partial to a little hors d'oeuvre of historical background, so I can tell you that the area was once an ancient site for prominent Irish chieftains. Presbyterian settlers built the current

51

town in the 1600's, 'a plantation town', as we politely say in these times of political correctness. There are a considerable number of Anglo-Irish estates built on the periphery. The settlers apparently enticed by the fertility of the land and the abundance of the river...or yadi, yadi, yadi... by order of Queen Elizabeth or James the First or whatever, whoever was land gabbing at the time. I can't really think of people wanting to move here by choice. But let's try to keep our personal prejudices out of our little tour and continue.

Yes, the danger must be growing, For the rowers keep on rowing, And they're certainly not showing, Any signs that they are slowing,

An inventory of amenities in 1987 finds the town well equipped with most neoteric conveniences; that's a bank, a doctor's surgery, a chemist and a butchers to me and your good plebeian selves. The town has two grocery shops, one is catholic owned and the other of pro-testant propriety. And when it comes to spending out hard earned crust, we all know which side our bread is buttered on!

No *Irish eyes are smiling* tour would be complete without reference to religion. Roman Catholicism and Protestantism have served to keep the population shackled to narrow-mindedness, in the guise of high moral standards of course. Rathford not being a place of any obvious religious division and this may be surprising, given its close proximity to the six counties border. I mean people are being shot at thirty miles away and no-one even bats an eyelid! If it is not in Old Moore's Almanac then it doesn't merit discussion. Watching Australian soaps had become the most popular pastime of our zombified inhabitants. You can walk through the town at 1.25pm and hear the grating *Neighbours* theme tune blaring from every window and not a being on the streets! *This town, is coming like a ghost town*...in my opinion would be a more appropriate anthem for the place!

Not a speck of light is showing, So the danger must be growing, Are the fires of Hell a–glowing, Is the grisly reaper mowing.

Okay my head is pounding somewhat so could somebody please cue some soft music because in the evening, la, lala, la, as the day begins to fade, and the lights twinkle on one-by-one, you can see several churches gracefully adorn the twilight silhouette, like a bloody pop-up Christmas card. Oh and of course, like most small Irish towns there are bars and pubs galore.

Oh little town of Rathford is like a glow-worm that eats into your brain, gnawing and tunnelling, dominating everything that you can or can't do.

And sadly our tour is coming to an end and brings us to this miserable little graveside of Lauren Doherty, an insignificant little speck *in the vale in whose bosom the bright waters meet.* Lauren, you see, knew only too well that small towns exist within their own boundaries and are answerable to no-one. And for her the only way to side step their cruelty was to leave. She discovered this in a moment of pissing and vomiting all her torture onto her kitchen floor. Her story would be spoken of only in hushed tones. A tut-tuting sound accompanying shaking heads, people exacerbated with disbelief, aghast in some pretence of shock and caring.

There are so many points of reference that could begin to give you an explanation as to why she had come to this place of no hope, so many reasons why she believed that she had no other alternative, so many starting posts, so many little beads of memory that chain together her life. Little beads of opportunity that were taken from her one by one until her rosary became a hollow refrain, until in others eyes she was nothing, nobody, not even a shadow on the beautiful landscape.

So there ends our informative tour and my advice to you is that you should blink and move on as quickly as you possibly can. In fact run for the hills and make an exit akin to that of a cat with its tail on fire.

They're coming to get you...haha hehe!'

Book IV

Rathford, County Donegal
1987

Hush now don't you cry!

The morning of Lauren's disappearance was different to every morning in her life for probably close on sixteen years. Lauren made it into the kitchen to prepare breakfast, which was usual, but without realising it she had broken a habit, a deep rooted pattern that had numbed her existence for too many years.

The kitchen was cold, the dishevelment and aged furniture didn't help the coldness but Lauren was used to it, she rarely noticed it anymore for the place never felt like it belonged to her to begin with. Lauren lifted an enamelled saucepan from the cupboard and was about to add the oatmeal when she paused, because a random little culprit of a thought entered her mind that had been savagely muted.

Lauren remembered that she hadn't taken her medication the night before, yet she had had the best night's sleep for years and when she woke up she had felt energised. Lauren couldn't remember where Daddy had put her tablets and she quickly turned to panic and became confused. Lauren began to shake; her body reacting to the anxiety by going into some kind of a fit. Her heart pounded and the muscles tensed and strained and it filled her ears, like the sound of someone hammering in a fence post and the noise resonates and pulses about the landscape so that you don't know where the original sound comes from.

Lauren had no way of controlling what was happening. She had no way of holding everything inside anymore. All of her senses flushed and a warm sweat began to ooze from every pore and this made her feel alive, ecstatic like some religious visionary about to receive a message from the divine.

Lauren willingly let herself go and began to relax and enjoy the warmth of being overwhelmed, like when you can laugh and cry at the same time, but you're not sure which you want to do the most, because each is giving you equal pleasure.

I can see her…I can see her clearly…I know I have to create a memory of her because there is no way I can know exactly what happened…but I am with her.

'Sshhh…Lauren, it's Adele! I'm back…I'm here to help you! *Too-ra-loo-ra-loo-ral, Too-ra-loo-ra-li, Too-ra-loo-ra-loo-ral, hush now, don't you cry*!'

I don't have to get upset when I see her cosseted and cradled. I can be with her and she isn't all alone in the world. I can tell her not to be afraid.

'It's me Lauren. I'm here with you.'

I need to see her so I know what she told me is true. I need her despair to be in my head. Romantic Ireland's alive and well in sentimental piss, *too-ra-loo-ra-loo-ra, that's an Irish lullaby!*

The euphoria envelopes Lauren and she isn't going to resist. She feels uplifted. She knows what it was like to be free. Lauren embraces the feeling of not being herself anymore. She embraces the simple thought that she can just float away burdenless from her life. La, la, la, la, la, into the ether!

Imagine what it must be like to be above the fog…to be able to see that all below it doesn't matter anymore!

Lauren felt a sudden pull of consciousness like the way a bell ringer jerks a rope. She began to struggle, her body jumped, but she didn't want to wake up, she didn't want to go back into her body. And that was her moment, stupid as it seems, for that was the moment she became determined not to continue living with the terrible way her life had become.

At thirty three years old Lauren had witnessed herself as she really was, seen herself for the first time in a long time and it made her feel sick, disgusted. Lauren's moment of insight was to become her point of no return…and she knew what she had to do, she just didn't know how she was going to do it yet.

Then it was over, the faint passed, her eyes blinked slowly and she began to regain focus. The pit of her stomach retched, but she continued to lie, shivering, skeletal in a pool of her own vomit and urine…yet she couldn't cry for there were no tears, nothing but surrender in her heart, and that is when I found her. Lauren was so small and fragile I felt as if I could have lifted her, scooped her into my hands, like a pathetic rag doll that had been ripped apart.

Lauren had had her moment of clarity and reached her point of no return but for me what happened next would never ever be clear and in that moment all I knew was that I was trying to help her…it felt like I was helping her and I would do what she needed me to do so that she wouldn't hurt anymore.

I would spend years going over that last morning with Lauren in my head until it became worn and ragged and I can no longer see it in sequence, memories inserted and deleted, like an writer struggling to put together a coherent paragraph. I still desperately want to be with her on that day, knowing what I know now, understanding better what I couldn't understand then.

When I was a wee wain I used to scour the fields looking for a four leaf clover that would grant me three wishes. Three wishes didn't seem like a lot to ask for. Three wishes could undo the curse of our lives. Its madness how so many of us want to change what we were born into…to have the ability to just wish it all away…*star light, star bright, the first star I see tonight, I wish I may, I wish I might, have the wish I make tonight*…and in the end I suppose you think about what you can put in your head to replace the gross images. You think about what you can sing or say that will make them go away. You think about lullabies and poems and stories so that the truth can curl like fog into the subtext.

All the king's horses and all the king's…

I had skipped towards the kitchen that morning with teenage oblivion. I was rehearsing something in my head. I had been looking forward to something that day, but I don't remember what it was now and it doesn't matter anymore because it all disappeared, vanished in the moment that I was about to enter the kitchen.

I stopped dumbstruck in the doorway. I had found Lauren before on many an occasion, curled up and crying. But that was usually after Daddy had beaten her and that was what I first thought had happened. But something felt different; my instinct told me that something terrible was wrong. Lauren wasn't moving and the smell of urine was heavy and nauseating and I felt heavy and nauseated. My legs wobbled but I steadied them, leaning defeated against the doorframe.

Not again, I thought, please God not again.

'Lauren.'

I said her name gently, but I was still unable to move.

'Please, please Lauren you have got to get up.' But my voice wasn't loud and I knew that she couldn't hear me.

I don't know how much time had passed, I was frightened, maybe he had managed to kill her this time, maybe he had gone too far…maybe he had finally done what he had threatened to do all these years.

'I'll fucking kill you, you ugly little fucking bitch! You no good piece of shit! I'll fucking teach you to speak back, I can throw you onto the street where you belong…this is *my* house remember…*my* house…do you hear me…nobody will tell me what to do in *my* house.'

Joseph Doherty owns this house, nobody dare turn a word in his mouth!

I put my hands over my ears, I couldn't get his voice out of my head.

'Shut up, shut up, just shut up…I can deal with this…I can help her...I can help her...'

I said this over and over in my head,

'I can help her, I can help her.'

I was trying to gather courage but I turned my face away from her. Why did he do this to her? I couldn't remember Lauren once speaking back to him and it didn't matter, it didn't mean anything to him. He still did terrible things to her.

I took a deep breath and let it out slowly and tried to gather my courage. I walked back into the narrow hallway and turning quietly went into the living room. I lifted a crocheted blanket from a battered chair, everything in the house was torn and bruised and long passed its sell-by date.

This time I managed to go into the kitchen. I just kept moving and didn't think about it. I placed the blanket over Lauren and began begging her to get up, softly at first and then with more urgency until I didn't know or care what I was saying. I suddenly felt frantic. I just needed to know that Lauren was alive. I just needed to get her to move.

'Lauren you have to move, Lauren please, please!'

I could hear my brothers and sisters shuffling upstairs and this filled me with even more panic, I didn't want them to see her like this.

'Please, please wake up, I'll help you, just move before the others come down stairs, please Lauren get up, please Lauren wake up. They can't see you like this...please Lauren, please?'

Lauren stirred and moaned weakly. I was relieved to hear her make any sound. She opened her eyes and looked at me but there was no life in her eyes. Lauren was disorientated, lost, and I knew she didn't recognise me, she didn't know who I was, she seemed to be trying to focus on someone else and it wasn't me.

'Where are you?' she said.

'I'm here Lauren right beside you!'

I spoke like I was a mother trying to soothe her sick wain. But Lauren was disappointed. I could read the annoyance in her face. She was hoping for someone else, like there was only one person she wanted to see in that moment of time.

'Come with me.'

Again my voice was gentle, reassuring.

I tried to lift her, but she felt surprisingly heavy and I had to let her fall down again.

'Please Lauren, you have to get up.'

She began to move but her body was anchored. I reached for her gently but firmly this time under each of her bony armpits and heaved. This time she helped me and propelled herself forward. I had her standing upright but I knew if I let go she would fall over again.

'Go into the living room,' I said.

I felt like I was leading her to the gallows, that she was some prisoner whose only crime had been getting caught up in somebody else's cruel web of deceit, she had become the fall guy, the scapegoat that had been easy to fit up. But none of that mattered, the why or the when or the who. I just somehow knew that there would be no last minute reprieve.

I could see the scene in my head. Lauren is standing in the dock, she has a black lace veil covering her face and Daddy watches unmoved from the public gallery. As soon as the judge firmly slams down his gavel and declares 'guilty' as loud as he can, Daddy stands up and heartily breaks into song.

The judge says stand up boy and dry up your tears. You're sentenced to Dartmoor for twenty-one years. So dry up your tears girl and kiss me goodbye. The best friends must part, so must you and I.

Everyone in the courtroom stands up and sways as they gallantly join him in the chorus.

I lead her into the darkness of the living room, the curtains were still closed and I laid her down flat on the couch. The dying fire

60

in the small tiled fireplace smouldered ineffectually. The last few cinders struggled to keep their glow among the ashes that finely powdered the air.

'Please, you have to stay here, I'll put the wains out to school, now…stay here, I'll get everything sorted.'

She pulled the blanket tightly around herself. I didn't think she would be able to move but I walked backwards out of the room. I didn't take my eyes off her until the door was shut tight. I had just managed to close the door when the entourage started to stampede down the stairs and on through to the kitchen.

Three for a girl and four for a boy

Karen, my sister, is on the rung below me in the descending sibling running order. She was the first one down the narrow stairs and almost bumped into me in the hallway as I quickly moved into the kitchen.

Karen was finely built and an astute fourteen and half year old and way smarter than most people I know. She always seemed to know the right thing to do and was precise when it came to making decisions. She was quick thinking and figured things out with ease. She seemed more comfortable in the world than I was, more practical and adept.

Part of me wished it had been Karen had who found Lauren. She would have acted differently to me. I was a complete disaster.

'Can't do a 'hate' right that one, you ask her to do a simple task and you have twice the work to do by the time she messes it up…you'd be as well to do it yourself…far easier in the end up…far, far easier.'

Karen opened the gloomy kitchen curtains, forcing them as they shunted on the rail.

'Where's Mammy?' She asked with ease.

'She's not feeling the best,' I said.

Karen looked at me with knowing suspicion.

'Neill is still in bed, you better shout him.' This time her voice was not so relaxed.

'Okay.' I said. But my answer was forced and made me cough revealingly at the same time.

I moved to the bottom of the stairs and shouted something…the same words that Lauren had used morning after school morning, year after year, but it must have been appropriate, for within seconds, a sleepy boy of twelve waved to me from the top of the stairs.

Time moved slowly, but then time in memories always does. When I see that morning in my head it plods past, freeze-frame by freeze-frame, second by sad second. The most enduring picture I would have of all my siblings.

Elizabeth is six years old. She is softly brushing her unwashed hair so that it flattens greasily onto her head. This makes her head look too big for her body. Elizabeth is totally unaware of how she looks, not even hot water could wash the neglect from her skin.

Patrick, soon to be seven, is chattering incessantly to Elizabeth. He is full of stories, always inventing mad adventures. Elizabeth gives him the occasional nod back, agreeing with his yarn. They are more like twins for they are the same height and were born in the same year. Patrick in early spring. Elizabeth in late winter.

Nine-year-old Marie, is sad and silently takes part in the morning ritual. She is like an apparition, a ghost child, a mournful Pre-Raphaelite painting and you could almost reach out and put your hand right through her. Marie is just doing her best to exist within her surroundings her, unaware of how broken she is.

Eleven years old Joseph, my Daddy's name sake, shuffles about indecisively. He is red-headed and freckle faced. He is packing his fishing gear so he can go fishing with his friends after school, or maybe during school hours, it was always hard to tell.

Sleepy Neill walks into the kitchen, last as usual but he gets there in the end, even when the odds are stacked against him. Pip you at the post every time! He is Aesop's fabled tortoise. He is broad and strong for his age. We reckoned Neill could sleep for Ireland.

And pan back to Karen again. Karen is watching me, gauging the situation without even realising how programmed she had become, how alert. She is assessing my posture. My folded arms. My tense shoulders. Acknowledging how I bite my lower lip or hold my head down. Karen is like a dog that reads its owner's mood. In time she would be the one to open the window and throw all the crap out. I would always be the one who would carry it inside.

But this was to be the last morning we would ever be together as a family. The last morning that we wouldn't know any better, a half an hour that dragged, churning drills in my worry, turning the soils of 'what if', and 'what am I going to do?'

I counted them, six heads in all. They were my siblings, tossed and pale, like her. Suddenly we seemed like Lauren, but with a bit more spirit, a bit more reason. We were the shadows that kept her going, the outlines that she traced but could never touch, the silhouettes of something that she had got lost among.

I could see the toil of our existence written in each one of their faces, the fear that we woke up with every day and went to bed with each night, the fear that not even sleep could take away. I wanted to tell them how much they meant to me, but I could feel a lump choking my throat and I couldn't spit it out. I couldn't say what I felt. I couldn't break the silence of our suffocated world.

We were seven pitiful souls in a world with no pity. We carried the responsibility and the ignorance and most noticeable of all on that morning was the sense of unspoken relief that our Daddy had already left the house.

But now, I just wanted them to go, to hurry. The crunch of breakfast cereal and the clanging of spoons resounded like an orchestra tuning up without a collective melody. I began to make packed lunches, bread, butter, jam, every action choreographed, automatic. I mixed dilute orange into bottles. Lauren had done it hundreds of times…and it was a physical ritual that was easily emulated…easy to present some representation of normality.

The siblings were leaving now, going to wait on the school bus, the school bus that stopped every week day at the gateway to our house. They didn't seem unwilling to go, they just bundled themselves into their coats and left. No goodbyes, no hugs or kisses, no see you later. I thought Lauren must have watched this scene for years. Why had I not noticed how tedious and detached it all was until this morning?

'Are you not coming, Adele?' Karen asked me. Her tone almost challenging me to give her a different answer to the one she expected.

'I can't,' I said. 'I need to make sure that she is okay.'

Karen left reluctantly, looking back several times; she made an attempt to speak but knew it was pointless. She knew what we were both pretending not to know.

I closed the front door and bolted it. Daddy hated us bolting the doors but I didn't care, he could kick it down. It wouldn't have been the first time he had kicked a door in.

'Yes, we have another door for you that needs kicked in, now this is a tough one today, a premium hardwood, but we know you're the best in the business. Put your boot into it there!'

I was just thankful that he wasn't in the house, for his presence could always be felt when he was there. A darkness like threatening thunder clouds that feels heavy overhead. He could puncture and erupt at any minute, find fault in the way you spoke, or stood or ate or breathed, and pick at your every expression, always a reason to shout or slam doors or just simply push you out of his way.

Maybe Daddy hadn't come home at all. Maybe Lauren had lain like that all night. I wasn't sure, but either way we were alone. Alone and pathetic, powerless little frightened animals, that suddenly were going to have to look into each other's fear.

In a nut-shell

Lauren was named after the actress Lauren Bacall. While her mother, Monica, was pregnant with her she had seen the film *How To Marry a Millionaire* which also starred Betty Grable and Marilyn Monroe. Now Lauren's mother loved the film but she thought that Betty and Marylyn were a bit slutty, so she decided to call her daughter after Lauren Bacall. She was elegant and graceful and deserved to be a millionaire's wife. Monica believed that if her daughter was named after someone so refined then she would make something of herself in the world. It was a name that deserved attention. But Monica's sentimental bullshit reasoning was just another miserable example of how we take our failed aspirations and hoist the responsibility for them onto someone else's shoulders.

Lauren was never going to be anything special for she was fragile and sensitive and far too trusting.

Come all ye maidens young and fair, all ye that are blooming in your prime, always beware, and keep your garden fair, let no man steal away your thyme...

Everything about her was minute and timid. Her features were small, her nose, her mouth and her hands and she was just about five feet in height. Lauren had beautiful, soft, long mousy brown hair that came down to her waist and parted perfectly in the middle of her head, casually draping either side of her expressionless face so that her ears were covered. Her hair had always been like that, even in the photographs I had seen of her as a wain, only now the occasional stray strand of grey had started to frame the front of her forehead, drawing attention to her startled blue eyes.

For thyme it is a precious thing, and time brings all things to my mind...

Women from the countryside had a tendency to look older. I suppose once you were married there was no longer any reason to make an effort or get all dolled up. People would only have said that you were shamelessly flaunting yourself.

66

'Would you take a good look at the shape of thon with her paint and her power clattered on to the nines, I mean who the hell does she think is looking at her anyway! There's no need for the half of it!'

Lauren's skin seemed translucent and had the whiteness of poverty, the pallor of personal neglect and hardship, a roughness that came from over work, worry and sleeplessness.

The clothes that Lauren wore were old-fashioned for her age, pencil skirts or black leggings and square cut tops that had been washed so many times their original colour was indistinguishable.

Lauren hardly ever left the house because my Daddy never trusted her with anything and he conducted all the family business. He handled the money. Paid the bills and bought the food and brought Lauren her medication and often he counted her tablets to make sure she was taking them. He preferred her docile, but then I never really remember her having much fight in her.

Then came a lusty sailor, who chanced to pass my way, he stole my bunch of thyme...

Lauren sat at the table for what seemed like a long time before she spoke. I had made her a cup of tea, for over the years I had learned that tea was an essential in a crisis. Tea, the drink that buys you time when you are embarrassed or hesitant and don't know what the hell you should say or do.

'There was a boy,' Lauren said, 'a boy when I was your age.'

'You mean another wain, a brother?' I said taken aback.

'No, someone I was in love with, I hadn't thought about him for a long time, but today I saw him, he was here.'

'When? I didn't see anyone...' But as I spoke the words I knew that what she had said was untrue.

'We went out for a walk...!' she said.

I felt awkward and shuffled in the kitchen chair. It responded to my movements by creaking annoyingly, and this only served to make me feel even more self-conscious, more nervous. Every little squeak, every little rattle had to be accounted for.

'We went into the forest again and we were holding hands and laughing.'

She sounded happy...youthful almost.

'Seeing him again made me smile,' she said. 'I was really in love with him you know. He knew how to put a spring in my step!'

Oh dear God, I thought, I can't do this, I can't listen to some stupid long lost love story. I had no understanding of love. Love was just some random word, like milk or bastard or pain.

Why could we not just clean up the outside and leave the inside alone, leave the inside to fester and hold the hurt. It was safe inside and we didn't have to acknowledge it when we couldn't see it with our eyes. We could deny that it was there.

'He has come back for me, I need to get ready, and you have to help me.' She looked at me but I don't think she knew who she was talking to.

'It's time.'

'Time for what?' I said, 'I don't understand!'

'He can fix everything,' she said. 'He told me how to make it right.'

Lauren drifted away again, into another world. She was far away in some ridiculous puppy love fantasy, where they believed that they would always look out for each other and would always want to be together and share time, even if in the end it was only a fragment of their lifetime, a clutched straw of respite in-between the toil of life.

Early one morning, just as the sun was rising, I heard a maid sing in the valley below.

Why was she telling me about some boy a long time ago?

Oh don't deceive her, Oh never leave her, How could you use, a poor maiden so?

Then I remember vividly thinking about Christ and how frustrated I felt when Father Hannigan read out the parables at Mass. Why did even Christ have to be so bloody obscure? Why couldn't people just say what they meant? We have this inexplicable need to keep things vague and abstract.

'Alright Lauren we can do this together, we can figure this out!' I spoke softly to her. I didn't want to confuse her even more.

But then even I am guilty of confusing things. For even my stories have a tendency of becoming distorted, until what has been said is nothing more than the tail end of a Chinese whisper, and if there is any truth left, it will usually be dog-eared and tattered.

'Tut-tut-tut, *clusa Madra, clusa Madra*!'

As we sat together that morning it was the first time that I ever realised that she needed something from me. But it was already too late for Lauren. She was so broken and maybe she was right to find solace in something that could never be retrieved, maybe that's all that she had left.

'We were in love… and we used to meet in the forest and make plans and we were going to leave together and travel and see places in the world that fills your heart with life. Places that make you want to keep going and see more.'

She was confessing a joy that she had held onto…a stupid keepsake that had turned into a souvenir of despair.

'What happened?' I whispered with effort.

'He left, his parents moved and he had to move with them and he promised me he would come back, that he would find me, but I never heard from him again, I thought he had died as well.'

'I don't understand, did someone else die?'

'I waited a year without any word, then I met your Daddy and within a few weeks I was pregnant, I had you.'

You have to sit on the blister

Lauren's story should really have been a straightforward and simple one, for her days on the planet should have been nothing more than a humdrum tale in the annals of life.

As a young girl she was just a run-of–the-mill broken hearted lover who met a man while she was on the rebound. The man was shrewd and sensed her vulnerability and he knew that he could manipulate her. So he told her what he knew she wanted to hear. That she was beautiful and special and bullshit sweet nothings and she thinks.

'Well this man is here for me, he won't leave me and he wants to take care of me.'

When Lauren met Daddy she didn't know how to pick herself up and heal her naïve heart. She just wanted someone to want her. Someone who wouldn't leave her and someone she could repay the only way she knew how…by surrendering herself completely to his every beck and call. Any kind of life was better than being unwanted for people eyed the bachelor or spinster with suspicion. Those who were left on the shelf must have some kind of want in them and taking what was offered was better than nothing. I suppose women were kinda like that then, subservience was written into the heartwood of family life. The core that supports a tree is made up of dead tissue and has to die inside in order to give nutrients to all the other parts.

Daddy was ten years Lauren's senior and he had achieved a certain level of respect in the community. He was considered a good catch and Lauren had been encouraged to pursue the relationship, it was causing quite a stir.

'Are you really going out with Joseph Doherty? Well heavens above, fair play to you girl…he has slipped through many a wan's fingers…keep a good hold to him now.'

The cunt was born and named, Joseph Michael Doherty during *the bleak mid-winter* of 1944. It was Christmas Eve and the

70

harsh sky overhead was burdened with drab snow-clouds and he was the only light in the world that night. He was a beautiful child, truly a gift from the saviour of the world. He slipped into the midwives hands so gracefully that his mother, Pearl, had said he would never cause her a day's pain. He was destined for greatness. Those who saw him at the moment of birth swore that there was a halo around his head, swore that no star ever shone brighter, swore with the sheer joy of being privileged to be present at the moment he entered the world.

And Daddy would always be embraced by all who met him, for he somehow managed to maintain the ability to make those in his presence feel like they were honoured. People revered him. They seemed to be immune to his darkness. Everyone and his dog had a good word on him.

And I'm off to Lisdoonvarna at the end of the year, I'm off for the bit of craic, the women and the beer, I'm awful shifty, for a man of fifty, catch me if you can, me name is Dan, sure I'm your man...

Daddy was a gifted man indeedio, not only was he a master at beating up women and children, he also displayed remarkable talent when he played the fiddle. He was the life and soul of the pubs in Rathford. He was a natural, self-taught musician, who had come from a long line of fiddlers. He just picked up the instrument one day when he was about six years old and began to play it, much to the amazement of those present, or so the legend goes.

'Would you look at the size of thon', I mean the fiddle is nearly as big as him! Have you ever seen the likes of that in your life?'

Oh he was among the cherubim!

Daddy played the fiddle with a short bow, which is a Donegal and Scottish tradition and because of this he could play at amazing speed.

'Wail into her there, go on ya boy ya, give her lilt-tee!'

Pearl had a scrapbook filled with newspaper cuttings of him playing at festivals all over the county. Trophies and medals galore!

He could 'play it like the devil at the crossroads'. Sending the devil himself back to hell with his tail tucked between his legs. He knew his jigs from his reels alright. Daddy always closed his eyes when he played and droplets of musical perfection rained flawlessly onto the listener. *Nearer my God to thee!* For like God it was magnetic, and it drew people towards him.

'You'll want for nothing girl with a man like that, you seemed to have turned his head alright.'

So basically Lauren trusts Daddy, believes his bullshit, gets pregnant and goes up the aisle hiding her bump as best she can. All the relatives are relieved that there is not another unmarried mother in the family closet, so they encourage the union. Everyone sighs with relief as the newlyweds step onto the proverbial hamster wheel of marital bliss.

'That's that sorted then…that was a close one…if you burn your arse you have to sit on a blister…in a couple of years time nobody'll even care that she had a bun in the oven…but there was a moment there at the altar I thought she wasn't going to say the words 'I do'… oh that's nerves for you…indeed it is!'

But for Lauren it was not going to be that simple, marital oblivion never happened. The whirlwind was short lived and it didn't take her long to discover that Daddy's anger knew no bounds.

The thrill is gone, the thrill is gone away, the thrill is gone baby, the thrill is gone away, You know you done me wrong baby, and you'll be sorry someday.

I have so many hand me down stories from all sorts of sources, sentences that people started but never finished, over heard gossip, comments made by people when you had barely exited a room, things that Daddy accused her of when he was drunk or in a fit of temper or both. Half truths, excuses and mostly a complete and utter pack of lies that masked the simple fact that Daddy could treat her however the hell he wanted, and nobody was going to tell him otherwise.

...the thrill is gone baby, the thrill is gone away from me, although I'll still live on, but so lonely I'll be...

The day of their wedding Daddy's uncle Pat was killed in a head-on car collision. He was running late for the ceremony and had been battering down the road. The reception was in full swing by the time the news reach Rathford. Daddy was particularly favoured by Pat so when he heard the news he was devastated. The reception had been called to a halt as people dispersed in disbelief and shock. Daddy and Lauren had gone to their hotel room.

...oh, the thrill is gone baby, baby its gone away for good, someday I know I'll be over it all baby, Just like I know a man should...

Forty-five minutes later an ambulance had to be called for Lauren. He had viciously beaten her saying that uncle Pat's death was all her fault because she had chosen the wedding date and if she hadn't had me inside of her they could have waited. Daddy said Lauren had put a curse on him.

...I'm free, free now, I'm free from your spell, And now that it's over, All I can do is wish you well...

Lauren spent the first week of married life in hospital, telling everyone that she had tripped and fallen over or fell down the stairs or some other stupid excuse that I had heard a million times and never once believed.

Daddy hadn't managed to get rid of me but it wouldn't take him long to figure out how to get rid of unwanted babies.

'We don't need another bloody mouth to feed, all these fucking wains tripping under your bloody feet.'

One time myself and Karen found Lauren on the bathroom floor and there was a lot of blood and she was on her hands and knees cleaning it with bits of toilet roll. Other things in the room were thrown about and broken so we knew Daddy must have done it. I don't know how old we were then, but Lauren said something about a baby and we helped her clean up but we didn't find the baby she was talking about. I remember wondering how could there be so much blood and no baby.

So baby after beating, after miscarriage after beating and she was soon ground into the dirt where he believed that she belonged. Someone else's cast off had become his burden. She had put a curse on him and he wasn't going to let her forget it.

'Lauren.' And he is dragging her by the hair out of the house and shoving her face in the muck. 'Lauren,' and he has a pillow over her face and she doesn't even fight him. 'Lauren, you no good whore of a woman.' And he is ripping her clothes and I have to get the others out of the house and not let them look in the window. 'Lauren, you no good little bitch, Lauren you fucking bastard of a woman, Lauren, Lauren, Lauren!' and he punches her and the world goes dark and I have to wait…wait 'til he leaves before I can help her. And I scuttle out of his way and hope that he doesn't see me.

Joseph Doherty king of cunts, king of bastards, king of evil men and I have no hesitation when I say that I unequivocally blame him for her death…yes, your Honour…your majesty…you most High Almighty God!

Book V

Rathford, County Donegal
Present Day

Full justice with a grand old send-off speech

'Jesus Christ,' I said standing up and shaking myself like a wet dog. 'This isn't you! You're not some ghost doomed to walks among their sins!'

'Today we shall master the art of standing tall among cretins, among assholeian plebeian, among those who take you soul and stamp on it and kick it away like a piece of rubbish because they only know ugliness and brutality and if they see a tiny bit of hope in someone…a tiny crack or a chink or a glimmer then they will snuff it out for they can feel only repulsion for anyone with a globule of joy in their heart.'

That's life, I tell ya, I can't deny it, I thought of quitting baby, But my heart just ain't gonna buy it...

I had returned for my father's funeral…one time myself and Martin rented a cottage near Lough Lomond and we spent a week cooking bannock scones and potato bread and eating tatties and neaps and haggis and we had so much fun pretending we were indigenous and practicing our Scottish accents and one day we went into a village called Buchlyvie and we stopped for something to eat in a pub and one of the locals started asking me questions about where we were staying and advising me on places to visit. And I lied to him…I lied about the location of the cottage and told him that Martin was my husband and when I went back to the table to relate my suspicions to Martin…he said to me,

'Why do you do that Adele?'

'Do what?' I asked aghast.

'You never believe one word that a person tells you…you always think that there is a hidden agenda…I was just watching you there…and that guy seemed genuine…and you come back here with it in your head that he is an axe wielding murderer!'

'I was just joking,' I said.

'No you weren't.' Martin answered me back…which was rare and he wasn't being cruel or anything…he just seemed worried.

76

And you know Martin was right and what he said stuck in my head. Why was I unable to take anyone or anything at face value? And the guy was probably a decent soul but my brain had been going sixty to the dozen and maybe it was just being in a small town again but I knew that day that I had never known peace of mind.

I gathered myself up and tried to muster a bit of enthusiasm as I headed towards the chapel again, puffing in and out like a train trying to gather momentum. I was on a mission and that mission would be accomplished. I had come this far and I wasn't going to give up now.

As I passed and nodded to the holy family statues, two mocking notes cut through the air.

'Cu-ckoo…cu-ckoo,' two shrill *I spy* notes called out to me. 'Cu-ckoo, I can see you.'

'Ah, shut up you stupid parasitic bird!'

I placed my hand on the tarnished brass door handle of the church and 'a breath in and a breath out…' and slowly pushed the church door opened again.

The same people that had let me out now had to reshuffle to let me in.

'All together now, one, two, three…'

I nodded humbly and apologetically making sure that the door closed gently. This time I remained in a standing position. This time I wouldn't make the same mistake twice. This time I had nominated myself as the designated gate keeper.

'Tickets please, tickets please, thank you, thank you…tickets please!'

I told myself to stay calm, fit in. When you tell yourself that you belong you don't have to listen to the panic. Martin's voice came into my head.

'Go Adele and lay him to rest. Leave it all in the grave with him.'

Ooohhh, Jesus Martin, for God's sake, sometimes you can sound like someone doing a cheap B movie voiceover or the crowned queen of Soap Opera platitude land!

But I would do my best to lay all to rest with Daddy's remains and knowing that he was a rotten stinking corpse would help me sleep better at night.

'And a breath in…and a breath out…!'

My eyes were drawn once again to McGroarty for I couldn't help myself.

'Lay it all to rest…obsession by Adele Doherty…eau de revenge!'

Slippery eel or not, I would get him in the long grass alright!

I was trying really hard to stop glaring at McGroarty…but he was the last obstacle on this road to peace and he must have felt my gaze for he began to shuffle in his seat. His movements unnerved me a bit and I wished that my eyes could laser a big hole in his fucking chest, burn his black heart to a cinder.

I needed to distract myself and looked with scorn at the people at the front of the chapel, the piety society polishing the altar rails with their cath-o-licking tongues. I began to think about all the wee dutiful women that it had taken to make the beautiful funeral vestments that the priest was wearing. The needle work was superb.

'Yes father, anything father…I won't sleep for a week father if that's what it takes to get the job done, father!'

The priest from dull-voice-ville continued droning. He was on some alleged heartfelt roll about the contribution my Daddy had paid to the community during his lifetime. How he brightened up so many lives with the light of his gift for music! It was a pretty pious eulogy. He must have put a fair bit of research into it. I could picture him interviewing the locals.

'What's the nicest thing you remember about the aul codger? Ah well you tell me that now…we'll be applying for a sainthood for this one…ach he'll be sadly missed indeed!'

Mad Annie's presence made my heart do a Fosbury Flop. She was nodding sleepily a few seats away.

Mad Annie the toothless hag, lives under a bush and dresses in rags!

Mad Annie indeed! She would be the one to identify me alright for she had a keen eye.

'Push me Annie, push me!'

Annie used to push me on the 'aul tire swing, on the beech tree at the gateway to our house when I was the size of nothing. She would push me for hours. Annie didn't care about time and I loved the sensation of being rocked.

'Push me Annie, push me.' I knew Annie wasn't intimidated by them.

The priest had started talking about Pearl. How she had passed away herself a few years ago and how proud she had been of her gifted son. How they would be reunited this day in heaven. If any two people deserved an eternity of fire and brimstone together, it was them!

A stringed orchestra of pus dripping demons tune up for the arrival of Mr Joseph Doherty, Daddy appears on the horizon and is prodded forward by a cloven footed devil wielding a trident. The violins start to squeal hellishly out of tune. Daddy puts up his hands to cover his ears but the devil bites them off and there is nothing he can do to block out the awful sound. He is poked forward until he trips and falls hapless into the fires of hell while a thousand demons appear and being to shovel sulphur on top of him and he plummets forever into his torturous afterlife, doomed to hear the violin screeching out of tune for all time.

Book VI

Rathford, County Donegal
1987

A good slap will sort you out

'Adele' it was Pearls voice, deep like a man's and with a hoarse edge that suited her face.

'Are you sure she gave you no idea of where she was going?'

'No idea, granny, I swear!'

I held her stare as I spoke. I knew she didn't believe me. I didn't know what else to do. We were sitting at the kitchen table, I was leaning forward resting on my elbows, my hands desperately clutching each other, my fingers tightly intertwined so that my fingernails pinched and marked my skin.

'She was always a strange one, your mother, you're a bit like her, can't get a word out you, like pulling teeth with a pair of pliers.'

'Mean old biddy,' I thought.

'I would love to pull her teeth with a pair of pliers, tell her how horrible she is, how gross and vulgar and repulsive!'

Karen came into the room, she was worried. Her steps were weary and she dragged her feet. Her demeanour was deflated and she couldn't lift her head. It made me think about how McGroarty had made me feel.

'Please God don't let anybody have hurt Karen. I would take the punishment for us all. What did it matter what they did to me anymore.'

Karen slowly sat herself down next to me. I winced tightly into my body.

The women that had flocked into the kitchen began to whisper and click their tongues and suck in their cheeks and make *tsk tsk tsk* noises.

Pearl stood up, propelling herself from the chair by placing both hands on the table and letting out a groan. She lifted a tea towel from the back of the chair and sternly wiped the worktops while nodding purposely to her allies.

I knew Daddy had been chatting to Karen, spitting question after question, trying to trip her up, he wanted her to get some information out of me and thought she would be a soft touch for he knew that she would comply, do what she was told, like we always did. He would have told her some sad story about how worried he was and how he only wanted what was best for Lauren, like the same tactic he had tried with me.

I couldn't look at Karen, I felt separate from her. So much had happened and I had been opened to a world that I could never escape from. I didn't want the same for her. But I couldn't warn her, I couldn't tell her about what they were capable of. At that moment I couldn't allow myself to connect with any one, I had to stay tight lipped...I knew I couldn't ever undo what McGroarty had done but I would never betray Lauren.

'You have to tell us what you know.' Karen said innocently, with defeat in her voice.

'We have to help her while we still can, while there is still time.'

'It's too late Karen, it's too late to help her.' I spoke with resolve.

'What do you mean it's too late?'

Karen's voice began to repeat what I had said; she began reiterating it over and over again until she became hysterical. She was shouting in a high pitch. I wanted to tell her to stop, tell her about all the pain in my head. I covered my ears; brought my knees up to my chest...I should have left already. Lauren had said it would be like this; I should have listened to her, done what we had agreed.

'What do you mean it's too late?'

I knew I had made a mistake saying what I had said. I had been stupid, maybe part of me wanted to prepare Karen for the inevitable, maybe part of me just needed to say it out loud.

But now Pearl was shouting at me also and she flicked the tea towel and gave me a wallop on the back of my head. The room became an echo of 'too late'. 'It's too late...what do you mean? ...what do you mean?'

But before I could gather my thoughts, before I could sshh Karen, Daddy came into the room, the darkness filled my lungs and I couldn't breathe, he grabbed me and shoved me into the hallway, then he reached for me by the throat and pinned me to the wall. My neck fitted perfectly between the thumb and index finger of his right hand and my feet hovered above the ground.

'What do you mean it's too late?' he spoke viciously to me through clenched teeth while he held his fist frozen in mid air, millimetres from my face.

'Nothing, it's just a feeling. I croaked as my throat tightened and I felt as if I was swallowing sand.

'If you know something and if I find out that you didn't tell me…your puny life will not be worth living…do you hear me…not worth living you piece of shit.'

He shoved his face tight up to mine; he was wide eyed with rage, white and bitter with anger. He had his best expression of fury on his horrible face. I just let my body flop, fall limp. Every muscle relaxed and I knew that if he hit me I wouldn't feel it, it wouldn't hurt me.

'Let her go.' Pearl had come into the hall and her voice had more venom than my Daddy's. 'Let her go I said!'

He loosened his grip and pushed me away with disdain.

I fell to the floor, my head hit the radiator and it made a dull sombre clang, like a gong, for it summoned everyone to come and have a look, but strangely I felt no ache, I felt nothing, not even fear. I felt like standing up and laughing at him, laughing hysterically in his face.

'That one was always whispering with her mother,' my Daddy said to Pearl. 'Thick as thieves...always up to no good...I swear I'm going to sort her out once and for all, no fucking wain of mine would go on the likes of thon.'

'Hush!' Pearl snapped at him. 'Don't be saying things like that in front of folk!'

The house was silent. The people in the yard were silent. Pearl was trying to take my Daddy by the arm but he shrugged her off intolerantly, squaring up to her before he stormed out of the house, cursing and justifying his public show of rage.

'He's under wile pressure,' Pearl said, shaking her head in disbelief, her eyes meeting as many people as possible, pleading and stressing for their understanding.

'Wile pressure.' She repeated it again, this time as if to reassure herself.

Karen came over to me; she helped me to my feet.

'Come on,' she said. 'We'll go into the living room, it's quieter in there. There are far too many people around.'

Granny grey will you let me out to play

The room was cold. The embers in the grate had long since died. A clock ticked on the wall and the pendulum danced contentedly to the beat. The walls were dark and the brown patterned wallpaper was stained with smoke and soot. An old sideboard sloped against a wall, displaying some dust-covered ornaments. It felt like a room that belonged to an old person. A withered geranium sat on the low windowsill and dead flies littered the ledge like mouse droppings.

My Daddy's music centre stood proudly in the corner of the room on a wee veneer table; its legs stuck out at an angle, as if they belonged to a new born calf.

His records and singles and cassettes towered against the wall, alphabetised. He always knew if one had been moved.

'Did you touch my records?' he would say raising a menacing eyebrow, 'did you fucking touch my records?'

I used to sneak in and play *Up went Nelson* when he was out of the house…I loved the noise of the huge explosion at the beginning of the track!

KABOOOOM!

Up went Nelson in old Dublin, up went Nelson in old Dublin, All along O'Connell Street the stones and rubble flew, as up went Nelson and the pillar too.

The thoughts of what I could do to my Daddy with explosives made me smirk contemptuously! 'Aye could you come here a minute and stand on this plinth, you know how much you love being up on a platform!'

The men in the yard left on my Daddy's heels, following him, scurrying like little school children trying to please the leader of the pack, gone to do their bit, show their good will and public spirit. Demonstrate how a community can pull together in a time of need, like stupid frogs croaking in unison.

Side by side, hand in hand. We all stand together!

I could see them, hopping from lily pad to lily pad in this stinking weed-choked pond.

The half a dozen women in the kitchen were motionless. The air was open mouthed, agape with anticipation, astonished by the sudden bust of violence that had rushed through the house and then the quiet like the shock after an unexpected gust of wind triumphantly slams the door.

'Bang! You weren't expecting that, now were you!'

The women remained stone-faced and had assumed a nondescript disposition in the presence of violence. Like an invisible visor protected their face. Then a few more seconds and the silence was ruffled by a cough and then a splutter and then they chattered nervously again without ever having to acknowledge its deployment.

Karen and myself sat huddled together on the couch in the living room. We too had closed the door defiantly.

'I'm sorry,' she said. 'He made me ask.'

'It's okay, he can't hurt me anymore, there is nothing he can do or say that will hurt me, I'm not afraid of him anymore.'

My hand automatically rested on my throat, and I let loose a few doleful sighs.

'Fucking shit head.' I laughed as I spoke and looked at Karen.

We giggled nervously.

'Fucking bastard.' She added bravely.

Then we were quiet for awhile, not really thinking, not really moving, not really looking at each other…not really knowing anything at all.

'What are we going to do?' Karen whispered. The fear in her voice made me apprehensive again.

'Just wait I suppose, just wait a bit longer.'

'But she's not coming back; I know you know she's not coming back. What did she say to you?'

'Ssshhh, they are all listening, they all want a piece of her now, they're all here to offer help and sympathy when it's too late, it's been too late for a long time, Karen!'

Everything was silent, and even though the house was filled with people, no one was talking. They were listening, listening for my voice, listening for the air to carry it through the walls of the house, to land on them like a moment of insight, confirming what I already knew.

Then we heard shuffling again. Karen and myself both sat upright at the same time, closing our eyes and shook our heads knowingly. The living room door swung open, Monica had arrived, like the pantomime queen, regal and dramatic. Lauren's mother, the other granny and she had brought the parish priest with her.

I suddenly felt bad again, my stomach fluttered, for there is never much respite when it comes to feeling shit about yourself. I knew I was a terrible person, I knew a terrible thing, a closed-door secret ticking and swaying, unwavering like the clock, determined to be heard. I did a quick sweep of my conscience…searched my sins. It was one of those moments when you need to know that you have nothing to hide, and if you do, then you need to conceal it well because the priest can read your soul, see the black marks, see you for the terrible, weak, ungodly wretch that you are.

'Bless me father for I have sinned…it's been four weeks since my last confession, I have bad thoughts about my Daddy because he hurts my Mammy all the time, he calls her terrible names, and tells lies about her. I want to find a gun and shoot him…blow a big fucking hole in him, I want him to suffer like he made her suffer…I want to…'

Monica staggered compassionately towards me. Her arms were opened wide and her head tilted majestically as she knelt in front of me. She had a languidness about her, her eyes filled with tears and she began to cry, for Monica was good at crying and she could cry at any occasion. Her tears were predictable, reliable,

87

inconsolable…she could make anybody do what she wanted with her tears.

'Granny, I don't know anything…I don't know anything at all, why does everybody think I know something?'

'Because you were the last person to see her, you didn't go to school yesterday and my daughter…my poor little daughter…'

Monica's voice broke off into a wail…she was weeping hard now, she had become the head keener at a funeral that hadn't taken place yet. Her despair was comforted by the priest, as he stood beside her and placed a firm hand on her weak shoulder.

'God will give us strength in these dark hours, Mrs Peoples. He is always with us and we must look to him for strength and comfort.'

Father Hannigan had many a well-versed phrase. In all his years of serving the Lord there had been no occasion that had left him speechless. For not only did he truly believe in the word of God verbatim, he also liked the sound of his own voice as he quoted from the Good Book.

Father Hannigan was a tall man and his body didn't seem to have enough muscle tissue for the thickness of his bones. It made his limbs seem like they were the arms of a digger and he could excavate great sods of earth with his shovel-hands, revealing anything that was hidden from his judgement. After all he was the eyes and ears of the Lord God Almighty!

Father Hannigan commands the lightening and controls the thunder! Burns the bush that you hide under.

'Yes children the wrath of God will get you…let's sway and pray and talk about the interesting shapes it makes!'

Father Hannigan's priestly attire made him look like the stereotypical grim reaper. His spider fingers made huge shadows that flickered like the flames of hell on the walls of the room, as he thoughtfully and meticulously moved his index finger to point at some invisible punch line that he had just expelled with haughty dignity into the atmosphere. He was a man true to his vocation, or so he believed.

Father Hannigan had been the Parish priest in Rathford for five years, and he was a watchful shepherd. He was well aware of all the shortcomings of his flock, the many needs of his congregation. He knew the challenges of his role, and he rose to them each day with strength and resolve, he had made it his business to intimidate and pontificate the mercilessness that God has for a wasting soul, for a soul that has been born into sin. Particularly within the Rathford parish and the wretched people he was currently among. I mean we were the leftovers on the religious food chain!

So Father Hannigan loved nothing more than taking charge in moments of spiritual crisis, we were fucked to hell anyway, but he would give salvation a semblance of a go! It only reinforced how haughty he was. How he laboured tirelessly in the field to fulfil God's work on this cruel earth!

'Do not worry Mrs Peoples. I talk to the people. I will talk to the child.'

He spoke as if I wasn't in the room, his voice clear, accentuating each syllable like a verse speaking prize-winner, an old-hat *Feis* champion.

'She knows that she can trust me…she knows that we want to help her mother and protect her mother's mortal soul…it belongs only to God.'

He placed his sweaty palm on my knee as he spoke. I winced and I didn't feel like I could tell him not to.

'We have no say over how life expires from our unclean bodies,' he continued unruffled, 'and if we think we are above the power of God almighty…' he paused again, his thumb extended.

'Then there is only one place that our immortal souls will go.'

He slowly turned his thumb downwards like some Roman emperor determining the fate of a gladiator.

People exhaled loudly and looked at each other with fear but there was no relief. Monica wailed again and Father Hannigan's untamed, huge, grey, bristly eyebrows stood on end, dominating his gaunt face. He was about to continue his speech, but his current dramatic pause allowed me to speak first.

'Father, please…I don't know where Lauren is, she never said anything to me, aye she was scared, but she was always scared.'

I spoke with confidence; no-one was going to intimidate me, not any more. To hell with them, they didn't give a shit about her when she was alive!

The wood for the trees

'You need to get away from here.'

My mother's voice called me back to the kitchen. The morning sun glared in the window and was low in the sky and its erratic rays bounced about the kitchen but didn't seem to stay long enough in the one place to offer any heat.

We had been talking for over an hour. Lauren was confused and didn't seem to know who I was...she kept calling me 'Lauren' and I didn't understand why...so I just answered her and pretended that my name was Lauren, and the more we talked the more elated she became and she seemed lighter for she had a plan.

'But where can I go, and why can't you come with me?'

I wanted both of us to pack our bags and just leave, run away.

'I can't go with you,' she said. 'There is only one place I want to go, and I can't take you with me.'

'But why Lauren, why?'

I desperately reached my hand across the table hoping she would touch it but it lay there like an unwanted offering.

'Did you know that I was the best wain in the whole school at skipping, better than anyone else by far.' She pushed her shoulders back and her voice was proud.

'I used to skip from morning to night. I couldn't look at an aul piece of rope lying on the ground without giving it a go. I could skip for hours...one day I did one thousand three hundred and forty three skips without stopping.'

'Please stop talking about things that don't make sense. What about the rest of us...us wains?' I wanted her to remember that I was her daughter and that she had more children.

'I've made up my mind about what's to be done and I can't do it alone. You are the only one that I can trust to help me. I need you to help me!'

'I don't understand,' I said. 'Lauren if you want me to help you, you need to help me understand.'

But she wasn't listening and I couldn't get the fear out of my head that she would leave us with him! She couldn't leave us all on our own with him. She just couldn't.

The dirty breakfast dishes were piled awkwardly into the kitchen sink and the worktops were cluttered and in a mess.

'We should tidy up,' I said, 'you'd feel better if the place was spick and span…if we get stuck in sure it wouldn't…' I tried to stand up, gesturing as if there were things to be done, but she caught me by the arm and made me sit down again.

'I know,' she said, 'that you love stories, I thought you might like that story…about the skipping rope, you used to sit for hours beside that aul wireless listening to all sorts of things and I used to wish that I could have told you stories.'

'You can tell me anything you want,' I said, 'anything Lauren, anything at all.'

I'll tell you a story, about Jack a Nory, and now my story's begun; I'll tell you another, about Jack and his brother, and now my story's done.

'Well most stories start with once upon a time…,' she said and then she stopped and looked shyly at me.

'It's okay…once upon a time is fine.' I reassured her. This time she didn't refuse the offering of my hand.

'Once upon a time there was this lonely girl and she had a baby in her stomach. Now this girl knew that the baby had fought hard to stay in her stomach and the girl was trying her best to keep the baby safe inside of her. Then one day the girl found a wee kitten, it was a scrawny wee thing, and it was so grateful to be given a home. At first the baby's Daddy was amused by it, he would make it follow a piece of wool around the place, but then he saw how the kitten liked to follow the girl and how it preferred to sit on her knee, so one day he kicked it…kicked so hard across the yard that he killed it. Broke its neck and the girl cried and the man laughed, and the girl could see how it made him feel powerful. That is when she knew that he would treat her baby the same.'

Lauren looked closely at my face as if she was looking in a mirror and studying her own reflection. She leaned her chin on her hand and without thinking I done the same. We both gave a half smile with lips pursed.

'The night her baby was born,' she continued, 'the girl was so excited, she went into labour…and…I think she thought that the baby would just pop out somehow, just suddenly be there. The girl had no idea of the pain. She screamed so much that the nurses told her to be quiet. They told her that she was scaring all the other mothers-to-be, but she couldn't be consoled and the man was so wound up. He was really mad with her, the girl was showing him up and he caught her by the arms when he was sure nobody was looking and he squeezed 'till her arms bled. But it was hard anyway.' Lauren's voice lowered again and she withdrew.

'What do you mean?' I said.

Lauren sighed and the defeat that she exhaled draped her, wrapping despondent around her exhausted body.

'What do you mean, tell me, please?'

'It was always going to be hard, you couldn't go against what the men wanted you to do.'

'I know how he treats you,' I said. 'I know how he treats us all!'

'The girl was waiting on the baby to come along. She thought that the baby would make everything different, she thought that when the man saw how lovely the baby was, then he wouldn't be able to hurt it...'

I love little pussy her coat is so warm and if I don't hurt her, she'll do me no harm, so I'll not pull her tail or drive her away, but pussy and I, will very gently play.

'But sure none of that matters now, it's all over and done with.'

93

I'll sit by the fire and give her some food and pussy will love me, because I am good.

'It's okay…keep going.' I said 'You have to tell me!'

'I'm not smart like other people, I thought I could care…and everyone likes to think that there is at least one person in the world that cares about them but I knew the man would destroy anything I cared about.'

'But you could have left…you could have…' I couldn't finish what I wanted to say for I knew I was being stupid.

'Oh darling girl,' she said as she brushed my hair behind my ears. 'Darling girl.'

And that was it. I didn't understand her…and her voice became incoherent. My fear was choking on her words. I was confused and the fog came and I went into it and sshh listen carefully and you can hear her speak! Then her voice comes and is soft again.

'We can't tidy up the pain, Lauren...there isn't any place to put it.'

Lauren was weak and that was the most I had ever heard her talk in my entire life. I lived with her for sixteen years and that was the most I had ever heard her say!

'So many years pass you by and you realise that you have done nothing more than allow yourself to be kicked around.'

Her body trembled, I wanted her to eat something but she refused, she said there was no need. The little bit of strength she had found she only needed for a short while longer. She was pining for the peace that she had felt earlier and I was scared and confused and trying to be strong for her.

'Push me Annie, push me on the 'aul tire swing! I want to hear the sound of the rope as it sways and cuts into the bark of the tree.'

'Heeheehee, can Adele come out and play today.'

94

United in grief

Come away O human Child, to the waters and the wild, with a fairy hand in hand, for the world's more full of weeping...

Monica was sniffing now, little choked back sobs of pity but I knew they were hiding her anger, everyone was angry, they thought that maybe their anger could bully me and scare me into submission.

Pearl had come into the living room, she sat on the arm of Monica's chair, balanced herself precariously, the chair groaned slightly and released a bit of trapped wind from her impact. Pearl looked embarrassed. My head was beginning to hurt and I just kept thinking how ridiculous little Monica and plump Pearl were, like a tragic female parody of Laurel and Hardy.

'Two women united in grief...oh the antics they get up to...has to be seen to be believed.'

Some kind of stupid tagline like that! But I couldn't think straight, I couldn't figure out how to get away from them.

Pearl was trying to console Monica, for she knew that Monica had priority on the portions of sympathy, after all Lauren was her daughter and a mother's grief is a terrible thing!

I suddenly wanted to be sick, my stomach churned and felt bloated and I put my hand on it and rubbed it reassuringly but it wouldn't stop doing somersaults and I began to retch until the spasms became uncontrollable. I got up off the seat and pushed past the women blocking the doorway. I stumbled into the bathroom and heaved furiously. Strangely, vomiting made me feel good like I was purging all of these people from the pit of my being, purging all of their falseness.

Karen followed me into the bathroom and gently rubbed my back with the palm of her hand in long slow circular movements and it made me feel worse but I didn't want to tell her to stop. I leaned my head over the hand basin, my hands holding onto the sides. Karen gently held my hair back as I ran the cold water and splashed

95

it onto my face, the coldness felt good on my skin…I swished and gargled some water in my mouth, spitting it into the basin. Now I was ready for action again. I would not be treated the way Lauren had been treated; I would not buckle under their emotional blackmail bullshit! Jesus I would find the strength somewhere.

'Let's go for a walk.' Karen said with sudden inspiration. 'The fresh air will do you good.'

No-one seemed to object, they just nodded and titled their heads and raised their shoulders up and down indifferently. Maybe they thought that if Karen got some information out of me that she would still share it with them.

We left the house, the sinking little house at the side of the road, foundering under the burden of all that had happened in it.

'Where shall we go?' I asked nervously, half afraid at the thought of being vulnerable again on some lost country by-road and half relieved to be out in the fresh air away from the interrogators. There was nowhere to hide!

Ready or not here I come…!

'Let's just walk, go up Mooney's Lane or something.'

'Okay,' I said obediently.

We held each other's hand and our fingers were loosely intertwined and they began to swing to the rhythm of our walk. I watched the music of our feet as they moved in time. I thought we could join a marching band and I imagined throwing batons high in the air and catching them and twirling them with poise and precision.

Our feet seemed to belong to the one body and they jutted out below our pale stick-insect legs that were dappled and dotted with ink-blot bruises, something old and something new and forty shades of yellow and purple and blue, distinct against our greying ankle socks and flecking patent sandals.

Mooney's Lane was a small by-way that cut off secretly from the road that led to our house. The entrance to it was well concealed. You had to know it was there and have a reason for using it. It was lined with dark green alder trees, thick at the entrance, standing like sentries. These thinned out after a few yards. Then you could see open fields and hazel wooded areas and some ash, oak and sycamore trees defiantly strewn in-between the trimmed hawthorn hedges. All the trees were bare, except for the ash and the withered keys that clung to its lonely silver branches looked like little brown paper bats. The middle of the road had a long line of tufted grass growing up it, meandering into the distance like an ancient sleeping Boa Constrictor, lazily digesting its meal.

'Yes, this is a perfect specimen and it will take a millennia in order for it to absorb its kill!'

The road itself was rough and uneven and pocked with potholes, a testimony to how rarely it was used. The occasional drying cowpat buzzed with greedy flies. The road led to 'Brier Lough', an abandoned little lake that seemed to have no purpose, it was sullen and deep, and of course we had always been warned to stay away from it.

'Tis no place for wains, if they fall in there, they're never coming out again.'

A rotting rowing boat precariously hugged the edge of a mucky haphazard slipway. The boat had been decaying there for as long as I could remember. Chunks of concrete had broken off and fallen into the Lough. The rest of the Lough's perimeter was choked with reeds and rushes and willows. The overgrowth and the undergrowth were dangerously intermixed making it difficult to know where the water's edge began or ended. The gravel laneway that looped around it was the only guide and sometimes after heavy rain, even that would be covered.

One particularly cold winter the Lough had frozen over completely, it was an amazing sight and this had inspired me to dream of becoming a champion figure skater. I believed I would have a natural talent. I could see myself clearly, looping, flipping and perfecting countless, never performed before, revolutions in mid air. Swooshing to a stop with my arms outstretched to receive my applause. But my dream had cracked like ice underfoot and with one

97

hard gulp I went under. My wellington boots guzzled greedily, drinking their fill of icy water so that I just kept sinking.

Karen and Joseph were playing with me that day and when I was finally able to push myself up, they both grabbed a piece of clothing that bubbled to the top and with grips of frozen terror they managed to pull me out.

So there sank my dream of Olympic gold and world champion recognition. The experience left me with a fear of water and a week in bed with shock, hypothermia, double pneumonia or some other life threatening illness of Monica's conjecture. That had been a good week on the drama front for her.

'Oh, my poor little granddaughter…that place is a death trap…'tis only a matter of time.' Sniff, sniff!

Like she really gave two damns about me? Monica only ever cared about herself and was always looking for a way to have the spotlight illuminate her, like some cheap haloed religious icon that you bring back from a pilgrimage to Knock. In this town you had to be a perpetrator or a martyr to survive.

But those walks are the only times from my childhood that I remember being truly happy. The only times that I loved the elements no matter what they brought. We had tramped that byway so often that when I picture it in my head I can see it precisely. I can still hear the echo of our feet and the joy of our songs. An adventure group looking forward to see what the lane had to offer on any given day, maybe a fox or a hedgehog or a ripe gooseberry bush, eager little children that disappear with sadness into the dusk of my mind.

Karen and I walked in silence until we came to the edge of the Lough. We sat down on a rock that was long like a bench or a low altar, positioned perfectly under an old twisted hawthorn tree. As a child I used to believe it was a fairy seat and I would sit on it for hours waiting on them. Fairies were supposed to steal children and I longed for them to take me away. I longed to become the stolen child and I wouldn't have fought them. I would have gone willingly to their underground world and I would never have told a soul about what I saw there; a secret Lilliputian land where wishes were granted and anything at all was possible.

'Who can help us?' Karen asked.

'Who can help us,' she said again with despair.

'Ellen will.' I said.

'It's been arranged.'

'How does Ellen know?' Karen suddenly had hope in her voice. 'Who told her?'

'Lauren did, she phoned her yesterday.'

'But I don't understand, how can we all go?'

I was unable to tell Karen that I was the only one going.

The Stolen Friend

MEDIUM DRAMATIS PERSONAE

ELLEN, exiled friend, daughter of Lesbos, Queen of Mercy.

ROBERTA, Ellen's mother, nurse to Lauren, Queen of the Bingo.

GRANDA JOE, Monica's husband, the invisible man he being skinny as the shaft of a rake, pike, hoe, shovel, spade or any idiomatic shafted implement in a Seamus Heaney farmyard glossary poem.

Ellen was Lauren's only friend. The one person in the world that was loyal to her, even though their contact over the years had been minimal. Ellen lived in Glasgow and had been there for a long time. In 1987 I could only remember having met her twice. Once, when I was small and that memory is vague and was reaffirmed when I met her again when I was about thirteen.

Ellen was broad and strong like a farmer's wife, but best of all she hated my Daddy and she probably hated him with more venom and validity than he had for hating her.

'Diesel dyke,' he would say. 'Fucking lesbian…that one needs a good rodgering from a real man, fucking dyke sniffing around my wife.'

There was nothing belonging to Lauren that Daddy hadn't spat on, not even his own children.

Ellen had set sail from glorious Rathford shortly after I was born. She had been accepted for a University course, and when she realised that she couldn't help Lauren, she decided she couldn't stay and watch her being torn apart.

So Ellen jumped on the first bus going in the direction of Scotland, she didn't care if it was a high road or a low road out of this shit-hole.

When my Daddy first met Ellen he pretended that he didn't mind her and he had even used her to woo Lauren. He did a fine job at endearing himself with her family and friends.

If Lauren had ever complained no one would have understood anyway.

'That one just likes to be the centre of a whole Hoo-ha!'

Hoo-ha /who ha/ *n.* a drama or sensation deliberately caused by someone deprived of childhood attention. A sound produced by a human pooch when making a reel out of a jig.

They would have just told themselves that she was hard to please or just making stuff up.

'Never satisfied that one, has it all and it still isn't good enough…you give her happiness on a plate and she'll complain about the plate!'

I knew only too well the kind of things people would say to avoid taking responsibility for a bad situation.

After Lauren married my Daddy, especially at the beginning, when he left Lauren on her own, he tolerated Ellen. I think it eased his conscience. Lauren had company and he certainly didn't need to sit with 'a couple of cackling teenagers.'

Ellen knew that Lauren was unhappy, she hadn't once bought into the 'Oh I walked into a door,' bullshit. She continually begged Lauren to leave, they could go away together, take me with them. They could work and share the responsibility of looking after me.

Then one night Daddy came home early and overheard them talking about leaving. He listened outside the door for as long as he could contain himself before crashing into the kitchen. He wielded a claw hammer and threateningly told Ellen that if she darkened his door again he would use it. Nobody would miss a dyke like her. Her kind wasn't welcome anywhere.

Ellen was forced to leave the house that night. Daddy got Lauren alone and was so sweet to her. He made her feel like it was the way things were before the wedding. He hugged her and told her that they didn't need anybody else and that I would soon be born and the likes of Ellen shouldn't be allowed near wains.

I suppose Lauren was still naïve enough to believe in 'happy ever after'. She was waiting on the magic wand of marital bliss to pass over them. She couldn't accept that at seventeen years of age she had a failed marriage. She still believed if she was good enough, pleased him enough then he would realise how much he loved her and start treating her right, it could be good again like those first few weeks when they had first met. Imagine spending years with someone and having to hold onto a few weeks of happiness that was all just one big ugly lie!

Lauren wouldn't go with Ellen. She couldn't bring herself to leave. She wasn't ready. He had weakened her emotionally and she believed that if everyone else in the Rathford universe thought that my Daddy was a great man then she just needed a bit more time. She was so lucky that he chose 'a nothing' like her to marry!

So Ellen left broken hearted and the two times Lauren saw her after that she felt great shame, shame at her appearance, shame at having given up on herself, shame that she was weak while Ellen had been strong.

The merry widow waltz

B-I-N-G-O, B-I-N-G-O, B-I-N-G-O, and Bingo was his name-o

Roberta became the link between Ellen and Lauren. Roberta was Ellen's mother. She was a robust woman, like her daughter, and she had known Lauren from when she was a young child.

Lauren and Ellen had grown up together. They were four years old when they met on their first day at school and a friendship formed. Ellen and Lauren became inseparable, and people often passed remarks.

'They are like two peas in a pod…you don't see one without the other…joined at the hip them two.'

And they might as well have been twins for they knew what the other was thinking and they liked the same things.

Lauren often stayed over at Ellen's and would get fed there also because Monica had difficulty with the art of fine cooking. In fact she hated it, hated the idea that food was gone no sooner than it was prepared.

'A waste of time food is, no sooner on the table and it is gone again…everyone is obsessed with bloody food!' Monica would sound off as her voice disappeared into a high-pitch that made all the dogs within a two mile radius wail and howl for dear life.

'I can't stand it, and all those people overweight. Well! I would never leave the house if I was the size of some people.'

My granda Joe, Monica's husband, the invisible man never left the house and he was as skinny as a rake!

Roberta was a rare breed in a weather-beaten-down community. She was a kind woman and was fond of Lauren and also liked the fact that Ellen had company of her own age. Ellen was an only child and when people said to Roberta,

'It's time you hooked up again and gave that one some company. You know the old saying, an only child is a lonely child.'

Roberta would just shrug them off.

'Sure she has Lauren, I've practically adopted her anyway…she's part of the furniture.'

Roberta always said that she had been joyfully granted early retirement and she lived in a world of daytime radio, home baking, flowerbed weeding, reading *The Peoples Friend* and the two evenings a week that she ventured forth into the world, she went to the bingo.

The infamous 'Bingo Bus' picked her up at the end of the rhododendron lined laneway and left her home safe and sound, precisely three hours later, to the very same spot. The precision tools of a mathematician couldn't have achieved the exactness of position or timing made on each occasion, as a bingo bus driver with his pick-ups and drop-off points.

The 'Bingo Bus' was laden with women in dingy coats that were too big and headscarves that were pulled too tight and knotted under their chins. The 'Bingo Bus' stopped outside a small parish hall on the outskirts of the town and out filed the women who wanted to win a couple of pounds so that the house keeping money might be stretched to an occasional luxury.

'Aye, tis grand to get out for a few of hours, get the head cleared and ready for action again...sure it recharges the batteries!'

Hair rollers protruded above their taut foreheads and this headgear along with chain-smoking did not impede their persistent raucous chattering.

I realise now that bingo was the nearest equivalent to a night at the Oscars for a lot of housewives in rural communities. One that women could partake of in all good conscience, for it was reassuringly the only form of gambling approved of by the priests in the parishes and probably because the clergy oversaw the events in their own church halls as well as benefitting from the night's takings. The bingo was a justifiable opportunity to leave demanding wains behind for a couple of hours escape and sanctuary.

The occasions when Roberta won were always moments to be celebrated. She would give the girls money for their bus ticket into Letterkennedy so that they could go for a nosey around the shops. The girls could go the pictures, or buy stickers or stationary or treat themselves to coconut macaroons.

Roberta let the girls 'batter on' and gave them a free hand. Even after Ellen left, Roberta was the only one to show Lauren any kindness. Sometimes she would still give her money from her bingo wins. Tell her to keep it to herself. Not to tell anyone.

> **Batter on** /*bat-her on*/ v. to carry on regardless, and against the grain, in the certainty of failure in the face of insurmountable odds (as opposed to '***On the Batter***' which indicates carrying on drinking regardless of mixing the grape, the grain, the *poitín*, or any other zymological concoction).

Roberta had also picked Lauren up plenty of times, but she was practical about it and you could see the confusion in the strength that she showed. She never told Lauren what to do. She never scorned her or passed any harsh comment. She never told her to leave my Daddy or judged her in any way.

Roberta never came empty handed. She brought Lauren clothes and food and sometimes small trinkets. She cleaned her bruises and showed her more kindness than anyone else and that probably included us wains.

But most importantly, she told her about Ellen. She relayed messages between them both because Daddy no longer allowed Ellen to visit. He had threatened to kill her again, the time she came to visit when I was four.

'You come here putting fancy notions in Lauren's head, I'll fucking do time for you…you ugly hairy dyke.'

He felt threatened by her and he knew that she was the one person who could take Lauren away. How could he ever show his face again if his wife left him for a dyke.

So Lauren wasn't allowed to have any friends and Daddy only tolerated Roberta, for even though he thought she was a bit crazy…she always brought free food and stuff for us wains and that meant less money had to be spent on the housekeeping.

'A silly aul fool always rabbiting on about nothing, a bloody 'aul headcase if you ask me…and we have too many of them here as it is.'

> **Headcase**/ *heed kayss*/ *n.* an honorific attributed to a person whose recent actions were of such blatant folly that death was a real possibility. The *Headcase* is unaware of, or uncaring of, the consequences of their actions.
> Research indicates a genetic link between *"what a guy"* thought *"simple"* through to *"headcase"* and recent experiments have met with some success in isolated parts of Ireland. Attempts to graduate from *"headcase"* to *"loon"* however have been inconclusive due to stiff competition in the sample area.

Daddy was wrong about Roberta and she didn't abandon Lauren and she was never intimidated into not visiting. Sometimes she brought us scone bread that she had baked, or fruit cake or fresh eggs. She would be swamped by curious children when we spied her at the gate. We would pull at the basket of goodies and we were never able to wait until she was in the house to see what was inside it.

Roberta was a Merry Widow alright. Her husband had died suddenly from a brain haemorrhage when Ellen was only two years old. He had gone to bed early, an unusual thing for him to do because generally he was a night owl. He would walk the fields at night, contemplating and evaluating whatever wonders he held in his head, over-seeing his land, looking for foxes or badgers or trespassers. The land was his and God forbid that anybody walked on your land without permission, now that was a sin that would go before *The Almighty*!

The evening he died he had been complaining that he was tired because he had pursued a local tramp for hours who he suspected was sleeping in one of the roomier hedges. Roberta paid no attention, for she was knitting a complicated, frilly little cardigan for Ellen and she wanted to get it finished that night. She wanted to show it off at Mass the next day. She just thought that maybe the lack of sleep had finally caught up with him. By the time she got to bed that night he was already dead.

'The sheets weren't even disturbed…I didn't even have to make the bed to lay him out in it.' She said.

'He was no sooner in that bed than he left his mortal body!'

So Ellen wore her new cardigan to her Daddy's funeral and Roberta always said it was a blessing having no man to tell her what she should do…no man to cater to. They owned a small farm and she said it was good to get a rest from all the hard work. Those first few years of marriage had been a prison sentence. She had grown up on a farm herself so the non-stop work was no surprise.

'Dawn 'til dusk and sometimes dusk 'til dawn, always something to do. Worn clean down to the bone you were!'

After her husband died she rented out the land with abandon. When a neighbouring farmer complained that her husband would be turning in his grave she replied.

'Sure he was always a great one for exercise most nights!'

Roberta and Ellen didn't need much to get by on.

'People want all the time.' She would say. 'There is far too much want in the world and want of the wrong kind.'

Then when I was thirteen years old Roberta died. She was at the bingo waiting on one number for the jackpot, she had only ever won a line or a house and she was determined that one day her number would be called and when her number was called it really was called because she jumped with such gusto, her heart stopped, she flushed and was dead before she hit the floor, a joyous smile still on her face. She died achieving her dream. We all knew that she was happy when she left her mortal body. She had in fact scooped a £25 jackpot. The bingo ladies agreed that Roberta knew that you can't take it with you.

There were rumours of people scrambling for her winning book instead of helping her but they never came to anything. The money was given to Ellen when she came home for the funeral. Although most people felt that Ellen had no need for it.

'Them that get, always have! Aye indeed they do!'

Ellen had come home, it was her first time home in nearly ten years and she held herself together well, but you could see how much she hurt. She stayed for a month and sold the farm. Again she begged Lauren to go with her, take all the wains and leave. But at that stage Lauren was so medicated that she had no will of her own…no clarity…just a redundant stare through a Valium haze.

So Ellen left again. Roberta was gone and Lauren became even more lost in the world.

The hedge jumper of the western world

'Let's go to Paddy McIntyre's old house.'

My suggestion was half hearted and I wanted to distract Karen, change the subject for awhile.

'It'll be warmer in there.' My motive was to get us out of sight.

Paddy McIntyre's house was abandoned now. Paddy had spent his life as a bachelor and was a bit of a recluse. He was known as the local hermit. People mostly laughed at him.

Black Paddy, black as yer boot, lives up the chimney, where he keeps all his loot!

Nobody in the countryside was beyond the nutshell of a rhyming couplet! Shakespeare himself would have felt right at home in Stratford-upon-Rathford!

'Pull up a chair there Willy and have a listen to ye aul ditties.'

Paddy was so black because he rarely left his fireside. He stank of smoke and was covered with the soot that continually blew back from the sagging stone chimney. The gape of the fireplace took up half of the small room that served as his living quarters. It was like a huge mouth and opened a portal to a world that seemed to mesmerize and draw Paddy into it.

People were always going on about him all the time. Calling him an odd ball and belittling stuff and would you blame him for running out of sight or jumping a hedge when he saw somebody approaching for he knew rightly that they only wanted to take a hand out of him.

'There you are yourself the day that's in it Paddy, working down the mines again. What year was it the last time you saw a bath! 1721! Hardy heehee ha ho!'

Bloody culchie ignoramuses, couldn't leave anybody alone without passing a smart ass comment that was nothing more than dumb-ass if you ask me.

Culchie /cull chi/ *n.* an unsophisticated and illiterate bog-dweller, usually ignorant as to the existence of cities. The culchie is distinguishable by excessive weather beaten skin and sun-burned neck. Their brogue is incomprehensible and most city dwellers proclaim them to be mythological creatures as they would never want to admit common ancestry.

Paddy would never have harmed a fly and he would just sit and stare at the flames as if they were telling him stories and what he saw and heard among them was more real and meaningful than anything in the world around him.

Paddy had been dead for about five years now and I still had high hopes in seeing his ghost and I knew that if Paddy came back I wouldn't be frightened of him. Maybe he would tell us what to do.

We used to visit him along with Monica. We always thought that maybe he and Monica had had a bit of a thing for each other when they were young. There was sadness about them both when they were together, different to Monica's usual upsets.

Paddy always cooked us soft-boiled eggs in an old bean tin that he skilfully set on top of the burning sticks. The smoke from the fire smouldered and filled the room and made our eyes bulge and crack bloodshot as we waited patiently for the eggs to be ready. Monica read the papers out loud to him and chattered away as he listened intently and guarded the eggs. Paddy gently removed each egg from the boiling water with the licked tips of his fingers and then put them into broken eggcups. He cracked open the top of them with one clean swipe of the side of a tea-stained spoon. Paddy always put salt into the eggs before he gave them to us. They were the best-boiled eggs I have ever tasted, and well worth the wait for they just seemed to dissolve on your tongue, like the way you imagine the Eucharist should and even Monica partook in the communion.

Monica never told us how she knew Paddy or why she visited and for some reason she would always bring Karen and myself with her when she went on her monthly visit.

The house had only two rooms, a bedroom and a main kitchen/living room. It used to puzzle me that there was no bathroom, but Monica had warned me that I was not allowed to ask about it.

'You mention that to Paddy and I'll make sure your Daddy finds out.'

I don't know if she realised the gravity of her threat. It worked anyhow and I never asked him about it but it never stopped me from wondering or searching with my eyes during each visit for a door that maybe I had overlooked.

'Do you remember the first time Lauren started talking tablets?'

I looked at Karen, and realised we were shivering, but we were resilient, used to extremes. I thought I would make an attempt at sidetracking, focus on something vague. I wanted her to talk instead of questioning me.

'I don't know, I know she takes them like but I don't remember when she started.'

Karen's use of the present tense made my eyes fill with tears. We had just reached Paddy's old house and I suddenly felt overwhelmed again, I desperately wanted to cry and I was fighting it, choking back tears until I would either let them go or vomit again.

'What's wrong, Adele?' Karen asked.

'Come on,' I said, 'we should get in out of the cold, come on…the back window's usually easy to shift.'

I closed my eyes for a second, swallowed hard and walked around to the back of the house. Karen was leading the way and with great skill because she was smooth and adept as a cat burglar, she pushed the rotten sliding sash window up, it didn't even creak. We shimmied in, head first, feet last.

'Maybe there will be rats in here.' I said.

111

The house had become a storage space for hay, but it was almost empty now, most of it had been used to feed the livestock over the winter. It smelled damp.

'How are you Paddy?'

I called out to him as we pushed a busted bale of hay against a wall and sat on it, our legs sticking straight out. Karen laughed half-hearted then sighed as she said,

'You have to talk to me Adele, tell me what you know.'

But I wasn't ready, I couldn't open up. It would be so wrong if I said it out loud and revealed what Lauren was doing. It was easier just to sit for awhile and to talk to ghosts.

They'll be time enough for counting when the dealin's done

My Daddy had come home early in the afternoon the day Lauren left. At first he wasn't concerned but he had been looking forward to a hot meal so he was somewhat irate.

'Fucking woman,' he said as he knocked over a few things. 'Fucking never here when you need her to do something.'

He stomped around for a while then fell asleep in the fireside chair in the living room. He had been playing cards and drinking *poitín* late into the night before, so he was tired, but not unusually irritable.

My Daddy and his card-playing cronies considered themselves experts on the *poitín*. They had hundreds of conversations about the bountiful amounts they could drink. The harder the man the harder the drink had to be. Or maybe it was the other way around. Then they laughed, t-heehee-hee'd over stupid stories that all sounded the same to me. They talked at length about the difference between the *poitín* made from barley and the *poitín* made from potatoes and sometimes even plums and how if you put a drop on a spoon and held it over a flame then it should burn blue, 'blue as the sky on a summer's day, crystal clear without a wisp of a cloud in sight.'

There was no wisdom in the world compared to that of an alcoholic philosopher, it was truly a gift from the Gods to be present and hear the slurred insights. They repeated the same aul shit about the stupid things they had done when they were 'off their heads'. Like it gave them a licence to do whatever they wanted. Like being drunk meant you didn't have to take responsibility for what you said or your actions either.

'Did you see the shape of Willie Joe the other night? Trying to get on thon aul bike and him completely legless, the tears were running down me cheeks, I swear to God I never saw a sight like it in all me born days and when he finally managed to get the leg over, he cycled straight down the slipway and into the river, it took five of us to pull him out, and do you know what he said? You'll never guess what he said…and him soaked to the skin…he said boys a-dear…I canny believe I came out without a fish in me mouth!'

They had the best of times alright and the *poitín* was a hard man's drink and they loved it as much as they loved their card playing. The two just seemed to go hand in hand, a fine marriage made in heaven and not like the fucked up marriages made on earth.

Come gougers all from Donegal, Sligo and Leitrim too, We'll give them the slip and we'll take a sip of the rare old mountain dew, and the fiddle wailed and *poitín* galore poured forth like a divine spring gifted from the very gods themselves. *Skid-ree Idle-diddle dum skid-ree Idle-diddle dum Skid-ree Idle-dum diddle dum day…*

The noise of the younger children coming home from school woke Daddy from his romantic Ireland *poitín* land of dreams, and now he was puzzled.

'Where the fuck could she be?'

I arrived about a half an hour later. I had nowhere else to go. I hadn't managed to get on the stupid bus and if only I'd had the courage to get on that bus like I was supposed to, I wouldn't have met Satan on the road home and...and…I must have looked a sight and I was numb with the cold and I could still smell McGroarty on me and no matter which way I turned my head his foul odour followed me.

'Where is she?' He asked.

'Who?' I said.

'Who?' he said mocking my voice. 'Who, who the fuck do you think?'

'I don't know.' It was the first of many lies that I would tell over the next few days. I was relieved that he didn't question me any further. Not at that point anyway.

As the evening began to draw to a close I could see that he was getting worried.

Karen had done her best to find something for us to eat and she got all the wains to do their homework. Karen was resorting to her pragmatic side, if something had to be done, she just did it. She never made a song and dance out of it.

Nobody asked him where she was, not one of us wains asked him anything, everyone was too frightened. We knew he was on the edge of an explosive outburst. The thunderclouds were charged and thick and ominous. So we just looked at each other, wide eyed and scared and tried to prepare ourselves for whatever the storm would bring.

I began to wander around the house in anticipation…waiting on a cue or a nod or a signal…I tried to will the universe to send somebody… maybe somebody would call in the nick of time…a knock on the door would relieve the tension…

Someone came knocking, At my wee, small door; Someone came knocking I'm sure-sure-sure. I listened, I opened, I looked to left and right, But nought there was a-stirring, In the still dark night.

I moved between the kitchen and the sitting room while loitering occasionally for a few seconds in the hall. I was looking for clues that didn't exist. I thought about telling him. I thought maybe I should try to stop her but I knew she couldn't be stopped and I didn't know where she had gone and even though something in the back of my head told me I knew where she could be found, I didn't want to clear the fog, not just yet and anyhow distress kept clogging my view.

I desperately wanted to have a bath, but even that would have made him suspicious and I wished that I could stop pacing about. I kept hoping he wouldn't notice me, hoping I wouldn't irritate him. I was trying to figure out what I would do and what I would say to people.

Finally Daddy launched himself out of his armchair and bee-lined into the hall. He picked up the telephone, paused briefly then dialled a number. I had no idea who he was phoning.

'Could I speak to Sergeant McGroarty?' 'Hello, Paul, this is Joseph here, I hate to bother you but…'

What did he want to speak to McGroarty about? What had McGroarty got to do with Lauren's disappearance? Maybe Daddy knew what McGroarty had done to me? Maybe he had told him to do what he had done to me? There was a pause while Daddy listened to Sergeant McGroarty.

'Aye that was a good hand you had, couldn't believe it when oul' Jonny, the man himself, pulled out that ace…robbed us all he did…he's a crafty one…he didn't knock back as much of the *poitín* as the rest of us though…did you notice that yourself now…he was up to something right enough!'

Again there was more silence…more silence.

Then he spoke again, this time his voice changed, he was trying to be casual but I knew he was worried.

'Aye, it's Lauren…I haven't seen her since I left yesterday…she was here this morning alright but…'

More silence.

'No, it's not like her…she wouldn't leave the wains alone, not on their own you know…what should I do?'

Alright, I'll see you in ten minutes or so…sorry for dragging you out…but it's not like her you know.'

My Daddy put the phone down but this time there was no silence…this time he screamed.

'Get this fucking place tidied up…Sergeant McGroarty is on his way…I don't want him to see this fucking pig sty…fucking woman…I'll fucking sort her for putting me through this shit.'

McGroarty was coming to the house. Jesus, I didn't want to have to see McGroarty, I didn't want him to be near me. I couldn't deal with McGroarty coming into the house. 'What if…'

'Did you not hear what I said,' Daddy bellowed into my face like a bull snorting through his nostrils and getting geared up to charge, 'I said move, fucking move.'

We scurried around, dishes rattled in the sink, clothes were lifted and school bags put into bedrooms. We just kept running around aimlessly hoping Sergeant McGroarty would arrive before we ran out of things to do. Seven lost little souls with more fear and terror than any moment of tension that a scary movie could arouse.

'No don't open that door…no look behind you…no he's in the basement...no, no, no there is no escape!'

Face the unfaceable or abandon the unabandonable, it wasn't much of a choice.

Then we heard it, the sinking noise of the Garda car wheels on the gravel hailing the Sergeant's arrival, an engine ticked over briefly then stopped. A car door opened and then clunked shut again. Our eyes tried to penetrate the walls of the house. Huge footstep crunched the gravel, he sounded like the giant that had climbed down from the beanstalk. Then a single official knock. A knock that had to be answered.

My Daddy went to the door.

'How are you Paul?' He said jovially. 'Sorry to call you out…but I knew that you would be the best man to help me sort this out…quickly and quietly…if you know what I mean!'

'Wayward women,' the Sergeant was shaking his head and absorbing his surroundings.

'Wayward women,' he said again fixing his gaze on me.

'Can't live with them, can't live with them!' He laughed at his own foolish version of a stupid catchphrase. Daddy laughed too but you could tell that it was only to please McGroarty.

I had sat down nervously on the stairs. Karen had ushered the others into the living room, then joined me.

'What do you think is going on?' She said. 'Why hasn't Mammy come home?

Daddy and the Sergeant went into the kitchen. They closed the door. I could hear their mumbling tones but I couldn't make out any of the words.

Half an hour passed, I didn't speak. I was wide-eyed with wonder and was trying to imagine what they were talking about. Where they talking about me? Would McGroarty tell Daddy that he had seen me earlier? Then I could hear laughter and they were both laughing casually as they emerged from the kitchen.

'Yes, well,' McGroarty said as he cleared his throat. 'We'll make a start ringing around and I'll have a scout about. Who was the last person to see her?'

'Adele was,' Karen said innocently. 'She didn't go to school today. Mammy wasn't well this morning. Adele stayed behind with her.'

My heart sank, nobody breathed and everyone looked at me.

Sergeant…major…general…field marshal…dictator

PHOTOFIT DESCRIPTION OF PAUL MC 'FUCKHEAD' GROARTY

Sergeant Paul McGroarty was a man of presence. His stature completely engulfed you when he stood over you. His step seemed somewhat lighter than his physique but he nonetheless fitted the job description well. He had mastered the air of authority, commanded the podium of superiority and believed omnipotently in his own power. He would uphold the law depending on who had committed the crime. So most people knew it was best to keep on his good side, which was quite narrow and only held space for a select few. Mostly work colleagues, and drinking or card playing buddies at that.

The Sergeant was a native from the rugged wilds of County Mayo and as a young man he was determined to be respected in the world. The wildness just wasn't in him. Joining the Gardaí was not only the opportunity he needed in order to better himself but also a way to command the esteem he knew he deserved.

McGroarty had comfortably completed his initial six months training with the *Garda Síochána na hÉireann* and was then posted to Mullingar in county Westmeath. It wasn't long before he was top of the heap with his arrest sheet and his stern uncompromising approach earned him a fearful reputation. He was taming the streets, weeding the byways and punishing the lawless, wielding his hatchet of justice and he was going to move swiftly up through the ranks. The Garda Commissioner had met with him on one occasion and told him that if he kept up the good work he was destined for the higher echelons. Words like Inspector and Superintendent had been used. McGroarty was reeling from the praise and fell to his work with even greater gusto than before. But the highway of ambition abruptly ended in a great big feck-off sink hole with McGroarty tottering on the brink of dismissal after an event in which a thief and local jack-the-lad had been beaten to death by McGroarty's well worn truncheon.

The thief in question was already known to the Gardaí and had been implicated in a number of robberies but they were never able to nail him in court. So McGroarty had decided to take the law into his own hands…because the law already was in his hands…so it was up to him to teach the young buck a lesson.

The young man was found naked and his body had been savagely beaten beyond recognition. McGroarty had gone too far, even in the eyes of those who admired him.

The Gardaí usually closed ranks when a scandal threatened their reputation and desk duty assignments were normally allocated until the dust settled on most scandals. The Gardaí weren't noted for squealing on or punishing their own, unless the entire apple cart had been overturned. McGroarty had certainly done that. He had brought a lot of unwanted questions to the doorstep of the Public Office. McGroarty was going to have to claw his way out of this one on his own. So according to the scuttlebutt of the Vitis Vinifera, McGroarty had to use inside information which he had accumulated on his colleagues to make a clean escape. It was rumoured that he rigged his relocation and his surprising promotion to Sergeant. An investigation into the incident had been conducted internally and the final record stated that McGroarty had confronted and chased the thief before finally apprehending him. Having hand-cuffed him to a railing McGroarty then realized that he had left his hand-cuff keys in the patrol car. He returned to the Garda vehicle to retrieve them and radio in the arrest to the station. McGroarty was reprimanded for being remiss about the keys and this was his only misdemeanour as it was documented that the radio signals were playing up that day and when 20 minutes later he returned to where he had detained the suspect, he found his remains. The thief had been assaulted and murdered in McGroarty's absence. The investigation concluded that nobody was ever brought to justice for the killing.

McGroarty was clandestinely reassigned and sent back to the wilds, but this time to Rathford in the far reaches of County Donegal. Out of sight and carefully placed in a small town where he couldn't get into big trouble.

McGroarty knew that as long as he wore the uniform he could not be deemed accountable, after all it was the first stain on an otherwise outstanding record and his hands were clean.

In McGroarty's eyes the move to Rathford was no punishment. He took his throne with pride and had been reigning supreme for fourteen years. He was in no doubt that he had made it all work to his advantage. To hell with a plain clothes cushy number in Gardaí HQ. He had other things in mind and could easily make a small town yield to his command.

'Good morning Sergeant, how are you Sergeant, fine day that's in it Sergeant, can I help you there Sergeant, help yourself now, take what you want Sergeant.'

The uniform was the seal of infallibility and you knew there was no way to get the better of him!

'So you were the last person to see your Mammy, young missy.' His voice was nasal, condescending. A stock of thick grey hair jutted upwards and made his forehead seem huge. His features looked like they had been frozen into position, like a Loonie Tunes and Merrie Melodies cartoon character that gets run over by a steamroller.

McGroarty's breath had a tang of whiskey and he spoke as if his lungs had to struggle to breathe under the weight of his torso.

'Well, I am I…I…I.'

'Jesus girl spit it out.' McGroarty said impatiently. 'I won't bite, you know.'

I was too nervous to speak coherently.

'I…I saw her this morning…but…she didn't say anything to me…she didn't tell me she was going out.'

I was relieved to finally get the words out. I wanted to continue stuttering but I told my mouth to stop rambling.

For god's sake stop dilly dallying…only say as little as possibly…they're not mind readers Adele…brick walls are good to think of when you're in the Village of the Damned…*I must think of a brick wall…a brick wall…brick wall…I must think of a brick wall…'*

McGroarty's scowled and creased his nose. I could see he was evaluating my tone, my pitch, my body language, assessing if I was withholding information. He had no idea at how good I had become at not reacting. But I wanted to cry, I desperately wanted to cry…McGroarty had hurt me and I had the right to cry. Then suddenly tears began to stream down my cheeks and I couldn't hold them back.

'I swear Sergeant, I don't know where she is, I don't, I swear.'

'Okay, okay, let's not get upset just yet…she can't be too far away.'

Sergeant McGroarty put out his hand to touch me and I winced backwards. He quickly withdrew it without having made contact and he looked flustered. McGroarty looked at Daddy. He could see that Daddy was annoyed with me, annoyed that my tears and bizarre behaviour was showing him up.

Cry baby, cry baby, Adele's a fucking cry baby!

The Sergeant looked at me again.

'Right let's stick to the original plan, Joseph, there's not much point in getting all worked up at this early stage.'

The Sergeant was only covering his own tracks but he also realised that if he did not keep things low key then my Daddy had his own methods of extracting information.

'I'll tell you what Joseph,' the Sergeant said, 'Get all these wains into bed, and when they wake in the morning…sure their Mammy will be home, a good night's sleep and all will be right as rain in the morning.'

What the fuck was right about rain? Everybody in the land was always giving out about the rain and now suddenly it was a good thing.

I knew the Sergeant had spoken for his own benefit, but I felt relieved that I would be able to huddle in the darkness for a while.

Faraway look and away in the head

What happened that night after the Sergeant left, I can only guess. All of us wains were sent upstairs to bed and we never spoke to each other. The boys reluctantly went into their room and us girls went reluctantly into ours. We wouldn't dare open the door again to peep out for fear he would hear us.

I hadn't eaten all day and I don't suppose the others had eaten much since their lunch at school. Karen had only found bread in the kitchen and made toast for the dinner. Nobody said they were hungry, or scared or anything. Before I put out the light we never spoke a word but we hugged, myself and Karen and Elizabeth and Marie embraced like we were never going to wake up from this night.

I lay awake in the darkness for a long time and sleep was a million miles away. So many sounds, words and images looped and replayed in my head.

The wind blew around the house and the occasional bark or chirp or screech protested intermittently, keeping my nerves on edge. I thought maybe she would come home, maybe she would change her mind, maybe she would just pay the price for disappearing for a day and everything would go back to the way it had been. Maybe she couldn't leave us after all, maybe I had made a mistake and it was just another loonie-bin story in my head. Everybody said I was always somewhere else, a daydreamer, not living in the real world at all.

'That one has the faraway look of your Auntie Rita in her eyes!'

Auntie Rita had left her husband on their wedding night and moved into the madhouse the next day instead. People didn't really speak about her, only to compare her to me.

What if McGroarty came back to the house? Would he hurt me again with the others in the same room? What if he done the same thing to them? I was too afraid to sleep, too afraid of what would happen if I closed my eyes. I kept listening for the Garda car to arrive again. I could hear Daddy's voice on the telephone and then he would slam the receiver down and then pick it up again and dial another number. This repetition filled my head until the room began to spin and I fell into an exhausted sleep and nothing could have disturbed it, not even dreams.

I awoke with a sharp intake of breath around 7am. Karen was breathing gently but I couldn't hear Elizabeth or Marie. I jumped out of bed and started to scream.

'Where are they? What has he done with them? Where are they?'

I ran onto the landing and into the boy's room. They weren't there. What had happened? Where had they gone?

Pearl came bounding onto the stairs.

'For God sake, will you calm down, I never saw one as dramatic as you, they went to Monica's during the night, now calm yourself down, we thought it would be better if we moved them, go back to bed, it's early yet.'

'Has she come home?' The lump in my throat made my voice barely audible.

'No…now go on with you, back to bed.'

I went into the bedroom. I fixed Elizabeth's bed. I began to tidy up the room, doing nothing really…just fidgeting for the sake of it.

Karen sat up, her face quickly grasping and adjusting to what we had woken up to, she was sleepy and tossed.

'Was that Pearl? Has Mammy come home yet?' she asked.

'No,' I said. 'Mammy hasn't come home yet!'

This is the café that Marty built

We were still sitting on the bale of hay and it was dry and coarse and made our legs itch, but it wasn't uncomfortable enough to make us sit somewhere else. The choice of seating wasn't the best and there was really no other option.

'What are we going to do?' Karen looked at me, her eyes were pleading. She was depending on me, trusting me, expecting that I would have some answers.

'Look Karen, we have to go…go back to the house, but we have to let them play their game…let them look for her. We have to pretend for a while longer.'

'Pretend what? You have to tell me so that I can understand.'

'Just trust me Karen, I don't really know anything…I just know that she won't be coming back.'

'Adele don't say that, please don't say that!'

But she didn't get hysterical or cry or fight me this time. Karen was finally beginning to come to terms with what was going on. She was loyal to me and I knew she could feel the fear and confusion. She gave my hand a squeeze and I knew she would stand by me no matter what, no matter what I had done or didn't do.

I suddenly wanted to tell her about what McGroarty had done. I wanted to rip the words out of my throat and lay them sprawled in front of her. But I didn't want to make the situation worse and I couldn't say the words, no matter how I tried, I would never be able tell a living soul about what McGroarty had done.

We left the old shack, the same way we had got in. We closed the window securely to make sure that nobody realised that we had been there.

My legs wobbled as I tried to walk and I suddenly realised that I couldn't remember the last time I had eaten a single bite of food.

'I need to eat,' I said to Karen.

'I need to get food. We could go down to the café in the town, I mean look at my hands. They're shaking with hunger!'

I stretched out my arms and held my hands limply and trembling under her face, we both just stared blankly at them.

'Have you any money?' Karen finally asked.

'Aye, I have money.' I said quietly. She didn't ask where I got it from.

As we entered the town people were staring at us. I suppose they all knew now, the rumour machine would be well kicked in. Nobody spoke to us. They just nodded their heads gravely as we walked passed while their eyes secretly followed our every movement.

We walked up Cooper's hill, a steep but small bray. Past the terraced houses on either side. The houses were all different shapes and sizes and squashed together. Some had been built originally to accommodate the dockworkers that had flocked to live in the town when the quay had provided a multitude of work. Other houses had shop fronts that had been boarded up. Most of the windows were draped with over stretched net curtains. These were stained and only added to the darkness that the houses emanated, poky little houses that lacked light and colour, sufficiently enough to dim and stoop the inhabitants within.

We reached Marty's Café. It was at the top of the hill and the building turned with the corner, curving onto two streets. We didn't have to go inside to be overwhelmed by the smell or to know what kind of food was on the menu. The irresistible stench of deep fried food blew into the air from a rattling old fan at the side of the exhausted building. Even if you weren't feeling hungry the stink alone would have made your mouth water. The distinctive smell of fish and chips was so strong that I thought I was going to pass out. Every part of my body wanted food.

We went inside and I could have jumped the counter but thankfully there was no queue. Things were bad enough without me behaving like I was deranged.

127

'Two fish suppers.' I attempted to say enthusiastically to Marjorie, the woman working in the café.

'Sit in or take away?' she asked as she avoided eye contact and rubbed the counter with a wet dish cloth. It was obvious that she was surprised to see us.

'Sit in.' Karen said.

'Coming up, now sit yourselves down girls and I'll bring them over.'

We sat at a table beside the window, which was a bad idea because everyone passing looked in and done a double take when they saw us, nudging and whispering to each other. Word must have spread that we were in there for I began to feel like we were on display in a shop window. The few people that came in spoke in hushed tones to Marjorie. Her replies were short and curt when it would have been normal for her to have talked the hind legs off a donkey.

'Aye…'tis them…'tis definitely the Doherty sisters…no, no hush…sure come back in half an hour and then we can have a yarn!'

The café had been painted blue and yellow inside, a vain attempt by Marty to brighten the place up. The interior décor was a stark contrast to the exterior of the building. You felt like you needed to put on a pair of sunglasses when you got inside. The half a dozen or so tables were draped with blue and white gingham tablecloths. A few poker machines flashed and hummed periodically in the corner, trying to grab our attention, but nothing could vanquish the thought of food from my head. I just kept thinking about how lovely it was going to taste.

Finally it arrived. Two large plates, piled high as a sacred mountain with homemade chips and the finest battered Donegal Cod. The smell alone was nutritious.

Marty's café had a legendary reputation far and wide for its huge portions of food and no matter where anyone ate after having experienced the portions at Marty's, the comments were always the same.

'Aye the food was grand alright but the portions were skittery compared to the portions Marty gives you! By god, one sitting would feed you for a week, feed an army...an entire troop...like Christ's loafs and fishes except Marty makes you pay extra for the bread and butter! He looks after the pennies that boy!'

Haha hardy ha!

I devoured a few chips with my fingers before I picked up my fork; I was too hungry to put vinegar or salt or sauce of any kind on them. We ate quickly at first, and then we slowed as the weight of the chips filled our stomachs.

'I do remember when she started taking medicine,' Karen looked at me suddenly as she spoke.

'I remember it clearly now,' she said. 'It was after Joseph was born and before Marie.'

'How do you know that?' I asked surprised.

'Because I was with her...do you remember...I think it was the second time that Mammy lost a baby... and it was only a wee while after for she took me to the doctors because I had got bitten by a dog...I needed to get a tetanus jag.'

'I kinda remember that.' I said hesitantly.

Karen had a great memory. I knew that well for I used to ask her to tell me stuff that I had forgotten, like rare days out or birthdays or Christmas mornings. My memory just seemed to be a series of blanks.

Karen continued eagerly.

'Pearl had an old fox terrier, he was ancient...he was on his last legs...'

'And you wouldn't stop pulling at him,' I interrupted. 'I never liked that dog, he was always snarling.'

'That's right...and before he bloody dropped dead.' Karen was back on track with her story. 'He bit me in the back, growled like a trapped animal, bared his teeth and he just bit me...for no reason at all!

She smiled mischievously, then continued.

129

'I was so shocked and it was so painful that I fainted…passed out and hit the deck and when I came too Pearl said I better go to the doctors. She wouldn't put the dog down because she said that he was on his last legs anyway…and the vet was too expensive and it was my fault for not letting it alone.'

'So what happened?'

'Do you not remember, that aul dog just circled the house for days afterwards till he finally dropped dead!'

'No, I mean in the Doctor's surgery?' I said.

'Oh,' Karen said smiling at having misunderstood me. 'Well do you remember Dr McKay, he was so scary, I was more afraid of him than I was of the bloody dog.'

We both laughed.

'That's right.' I said. 'His glasses were so thick and his hands shook and the nearer he came to you the bigger his eyes got. He always made me feel like I was little red riding hood in the room with the goggy-eyed wolf.'

'Well he gave me the jag and I fainted again, I must have been about five or six then…and I don't know how long I was out for but when I came round Mammy was crying. He said he would give her something to make her feel better. I remember thinking, why is she so upset about me getting bit by a mad dog? And he should be giving me some lovely pink medicine instead of her…then when we left the doctors…she went straight to the chemist. She got her medicine and she took a tablet on the road walking home…and I cried because I wanted one too. I told her I was the one who was sick…but I remember the name of the tablets…Ativan…definitely Ativan 'cause I've seen that name on bottles in the house since…as well as other different ones too. They all sound like the stuff you put on Christmas cakes.'

'Marzipan.' I said.

'Aye that's it.' Karen replied.

We had eaten more than enough and the food was beginning to make us feel bloated and sluggish but I thought we better head back to the house.

Marjorie refused to take any money from me, 'go on home now girls, away with you, we don't want everyone out looking for you as well.'

Digging the dirt in a flowerbed

Lauren got up quickly from the table. An idea had given her a new lease of life. She suddenly said with wild enthusiasm that she was going to contact Roberta. She moved with purpose as she went into the hallway to pick up the phone. I followed her, like a little duckling making strange quacking sounds 'but…but…but…'

I couldn't find the words to remind her that Roberta was dead, how could she have forgotten that! But then she stopped defeated, the receiver gripped in mid-air.

She slid onto the floor, slumping and sliding down the wall dejected.

'I just wish my mind would work,' she said, 'I can't think straight, I can't get anything to make sense…I can't remember a damn thing!'

She spread her finger wide and she began to rub them fiercely downwards over her despondent face. She moved her hands repeatedly in long slow desperate strokes that left pink streaks on her pale skin.

'I have Ellen's number somewhere,' she nodded to herself reluctantly.

'I have Ellen's number.' She said it again.

'I need to think, I just wanted to make sure that the man never found it, I just need to figure out...'

She closed her eyes and she was lost to me again. I began to feel angry with her. I wanted to shake her. I would feel better if I shook her. I wanted to hit her like he did, tell her to pull herself together and tell me what was going on, after all I was the wain and she was the grown up, it was up to her to tell me what to do.

Lauren looked at me suddenly, without meaning to and our eyes met for a few seconds and I looked away in shame. It was as if she could read my thoughts, my face flushed and I hung my head.

'You are not like him, Lauren, not one iota like him. I know now what I am looking for, come on…come on you can help me.'

'I'm not Lauren…' I said sadly but she didn't pay any heed to me…she wasn't listening.

Lauren moved swiftly and headed towards the back door of the house. I followed her outside and the ground was cold as we walked barefooted into the yard. The yard circled awkwardly around the house. It was made up of crushed shells and sand that had been taken a long time ago from the shoreline. They were well mushed together but I could feel the odd little broken razor shell edge that made tiny paper cut incisions on the bottom of my feet. I winced slightly and tried to walk on the balls of my feet for the skin was harder there. Lauren never flinched, she walked upright, more confident than I had ever seen her and I could hear the ground crunch resolutely beneath her.

We walked around the side of the house, passed the bright orange bottle of Calor gas with the matching umbilical cord that disappeared into the wall of the house. We passed the neat pile of kindling that Lauren gathered daily and broke over her knee, so that they were all similar in size and length and forwards and upwards and *onwards Christian soldiers, marching as to war, with the cross of Jesus going on before*…and passed the rusting barrel that caught the rain water that incessantly dripped from the spout.

The grass in the garden was fairly overgrown and tangled looking and had claimed all sorts of rusting and out-of-date farm accoutrements. There was an old tractor wheel lying at the side of the house, at the gable wall. Lauren had painted it white one summer. She then filled it with soil and turned it into a flowerbed. She grew geraniums and nasturtiums in it, but the plants were withered now and a soft frost, like icing sugar, coated the topsoil and the little knots of seeds that lay dormant on the surface. Lauren waded into the middle of it and began digging the soil with her hands. Slowly at first, then she knelt and began to pile the dirt around her, on top of her knees, anywhere, she looked like a child eagerly playing for the first time in a sand pit.

'Help me,' she said as she smiled at me. It was a simple request and she didn't seem to think about how crazy the whole situation looked. It was the middle of winter and she was on her hands and knees digging the dirt in a flowerbed.

I knelt beside her, we were both still in our nightdresses. The hardened ground dug painfully into my bony bare knees, but I began digging, like she had asked me to do, like she was doing and we buried the lower half of our bodies with a covering of wet soil. The grit lodged beneath my finger nails and the soil was heavy, but nothing mattered, we could have just been building sand castles at a beach or trying to dig a hole to China.

When I was down beside the sea, A wooden spade they gave to me, To dig the sandy shore. My holes were empty like a cup. In every hole the sea came up, till it could come no more.

I had no idea what I was supposed to be looking for and I pretended to know what I was doing just to placate her. Then I heard a rustle, her hands had found what she was looking for.

Lauren pulled a plastic bag out from beneath the heaped up soil. It was tied in a stopper knot at the top and she gripped the bag triumphantly, and then clutched it quickly to her chest as she paused, startled and anxious, she looked around.

'No.' she said to herself. 'No, no no, it's far too soon, it's too soon for the man to come back. We still have enough time. Okay Lauren, we can do this.' She turned to me with a big smile on her face. She sprang to her feet and seemed surprisingly joyous.

We went back into the house, back the same way we had come, back through the scullery *agus ar ais arís* into the kitchen, both of us covered in mud.

We washed our hands in the kitchen sink, the tepid water from the taps numbed our fingers even more as the earth ran and made a dirt track that trickled onto the unwashed breakfast dishes.

I looked at her worried, but she just kept smiling reassuringly at me.

'It's alright, I can make the phone call now.'

134

Lauren opened the bag, spilling the contents onto the kitchen table. Inside there was a considerable number of crumpled green notes, soggy and limp from the cold. She rustled through them until she found a piece of paper. There were some numbers written on it, the ink had been smudged a bit but the digits were still legible.

'Sit you there now. I won't be long.'

Lauren skipped into the hallway her hair swaying from side to side. She closed the kitchen door behind her. I tiptoed to the door and put my ear to it and listened hungrily as she whispered to someone on the other end of the telephone receiver.

Within a few minutes Lauren came back into the kitchen and told me that Ellen would be expecting me late that night. I was to get the bus to Letterkennedy and then get a MacLins coach to Glasgow. The private coach travelled the route everyday and drove onto the boat so I wouldn't have to worry about getting lost. The destination was the Gorbles in Glasgow and Ellen would meet me there. Ellen knew the timetable. It would be the same bus that Roberta had travelled on when she paid her annual visit to her daughter. She used to always bring us back sticks of Edinburgh rock in little tartan cardboard boxes and it crumbled like chalk in our mouths when we bit into it.

I had never been further than Letterkennedy in my life, well except once on a school trip, which had taken us around the Inishowen peninsula. Sister Geraldine had been our tour guide. The boys all had to sit on the right side of the bus, girls on the left and inside the bus smelt like jam sandwiches and I felt like I was so far away from home. But the whole outing was done inside schools hours, so it couldn't really have been too far away.

But I had told Lauren I would go, I had told her I would go to Glasgow, I thought I could do it.

'What about the others?' I said to her.

'What others?' she asked.

'Karen and Patrick and Joseph and Marie and...' but she didn't let me finish. She had no idea who I was talking about.

135

She just took me gently by the hand and gave it a reassuring squeeze.

'You don't have to marry him,' she said. 'You can get away from here now. You don't have to marry him.'

'How can you not remember the others?' My voice trailed off at the end of the sentence, 'how can…'

She smiled and softly brushed my hair away from my forehead as she spoke.

'I need you to do one more thing for me. One more thing...and then it will be over.'

That's what Lauren had said and it was the thing I didn't want to remember the most.

'One more thing and it will all be over.' Then the fog filled my head.

Book VII

Rathford, County Donegal
Present Day

Dancing in the aisles during the blessed sacrament of the holy Eucharist

People were getting ready to receive Holy Communion. You could feel the mood shift in the pews. Limbs flexed discreetly and people began to stir, trying not to appear restless, like detained school children that know the sound of the home-time bell is imminent. There was stifled coughing, repressed throat clearing, the rubbing and sniffing of noses, hair was pushed tidily behind the ears, chins were scratched and beards were combed downwards with the palm of the hand. Aisle manoeuvres were about to begin.

Annie sat bolt upright in her seats and was smacking her lips together.

This is the Lamb of God that takes away the sins of the world, have mercy on us...

Heads began to turn to the left and to the right in order to assess their neighbours size and agility.

This is the Lamb of God that takes away the sins of the world, have mercy on us...

Some people took a last check at their finger nails and then rubbed their hands together as if they held them under an invisible tap of running water.

This is the Lamb of God that takes away the sins of the world, grant us peace...

Throats were once again cleared and eyes bulged with the anticipation of moving their gaze upward from the kneeler.

I was fumbling from foot to foot to try to alleviate the fatigue that was kicking in. I was weary from wearing so many layers of clothing and felt haggard and unbalanced like an over dressed scarecrow.

Nobody was in the least bit interested in me. I probably looked like I had been given a day pass from the madhouse and it was reassuringly adequate enough to keep people at a distance.

'Don't approach the lunatic…stand back from the crazy…avoid eye contact or giving any indication that you are an easy target.'

I began to think about leaving the chapel again. I could go out and get a bit of fresh air. Reacquaint myself with the Holy Family. Pick a prime location for the burial.

The choir had started singing.

And he will raise you up on eagle's wings, bear you on the breath of dawn, make you shine like the sun, and hold you in the palm of His hands…

People began to redeploy, swiftly and adeptly forming orderly queues on both sides of the main aisle. All seemed choreographed and synchronised to perfection. People were well programmed and used to each other's circumferences.

'Left, left, left, right, left!'

The procedure was hypnotic and flowed as if a mysterious telepathy interconnected the congregants, nobody bumped into each other and they resembled a flock of birds dipping and sweeping and dipping again in the evening sky.

Mad Annie was on the way back to her seat, the communion must have stuck to the roof of her false teeth because she was sucking them in and out of her mouth. She caught my gaze and there was a beautiful moment of recognition between us. I instinctively raised my finger to my lips. Mad Annie gave me a tiny nod and sat herself down. She didn't look around again and if she had, she wouldn't have seen me because I was already gone. This time no-one had any reason to notice my exit for people had been too busy trying to pilot themselves satisfactorily into their pre-communion position.

I was outside again and me and the Holy Family exchanged a more casual greeting.

'How are you our most holy lady, isn't it a grand day that's in it.'

139

Book VIII

Rathford, County Donegal
1975 or 1976

The Pantomime

The town pantomime is in my head. I am standing back stage and I am about four or five and everyone is moving about with purpose. Everyone is excited and cheerful but I feel lost. I am unsure what to do. I don't know if I've been onstage or if I am about to go on but I know the organisers are looking at me like they wish I wasn't there.

Lauren has made my costume and it isn't as pretty as any of the other children's. I have a hole in my tights and I think I am a Christmas fairy or something. The door opens and Lauren comes in. She takes my hand, but nobody speaks to her. She has a bruise on her face and she is heavily pregnant. I know nobody wants to look at her and I feel ashamed that she is my Mammy. I lower my head with the weight of the shame.

We joined the Navy to see the world, and what did we see? We saw the sea, We saw the Pacific and the Atlantic, But the Atlantic isn't romantic, And the Pacific isn't what it's cracked up to be.

I can still hear the chorus singing with such gusto as we walk home in the darkness and the notes flutter after me and I am the pied piper. The leaves of the trees hold hands in the darkness as they all move to the rhythm of the song like backing singers. An orchestra of sound fills my head and the words swim and soothe me. The words stay there for days. They stay there until the shame is buried beneath them.

Book IX

Rathford, County Donegal
1987

The tell-tale phonecall

Karen and myself were silent as we walked past the Town Hall. It's a fairly old building and squats defiantly in a small plot of land. It smugly watches you as you pass by it. The outer walls are built from buff sandstone and are aged and tarnished. Parts of the façade have been painted green and red. The structure resembles a typical Church of Ireland but without the reserve of a grey exterior. The building is cared for and run by the privileged of the town and is shared by both communities.

The townspeople have a Christmas pantomime every year. 'Puss in Boots' or 'Cinderella' or 'Mother Goose' or some fairy tale title that always has Buttons and a woodcutter in then for the pantomimes seem to roll into one big pantomime. The same people play the same roles, the songs sound the same, the plot's the same, and the same set design is used year in and year out.

I never felt that we were welcome, not even when Monica or Pearl took us. I never wanted to be in that building and as we walked past I suddenly felt afraid.

'Jesus Karen, what are we going to do? I don't think I can go back to the house...I...!'

But Karen wasn't listening to me for her gaze was somewhere elsewhere and before I got a chance to finish my sentence, Sergeant McGroarty pulled up alongside us in the Garda car.

Then the traveller in the dark, thanks you for your tiny spark, He could not see which way to go, if you did not twinkle so.

The Garda car was dark blue in colour and it reminded me of the darkness of the water in the Lough the day I fell through the ice. The official crest of the Garda Síochána adorned the door and it was peeling slightly at the edges, like one of those cheap tattoos you get with the chewing gum and no matter how carefully you try to apply it, there is always a part that never sticks down properly.

Sergeant McGroarty leaned sturdily over to the passenger seat and slowly wound the window down. It was like watching a goldfish that was too big for the bowl.

'There you are now girls, come on, in you get…' he spoke as if beckoning a couple of puppy dogs.

Fweet, fweet, come on…that's the good girls!

'Open the back door there…and jump yourselves in, I have a couple of things I need to ask you.' The Sergeant's tone was casual but he was condescending.

I tried to grab Karen by the arm. I wanted to tell her not to get into the car but she had climbed in before I could explain anything. I climbed into the back seat and every bone in my body felt rigid and obstinate. We slid together until we were both in the dead centre of the seat. I wasn't sure if we were under arrest but I felt like a criminal. My head was lowered and I attempted to look around at the town. I felt downcast and wondered if anyone could see us? If we were never ever seen again would there be one single witness that could say that they saw us get into the car? Where was the fellowship of the busy bodies when you needed them most.

'Well, I hear you managed to get something to eat.' McGroarty said.

I snorted through my nose unimpressed and I didn't feel paranoid about his statement. That was easy information to get. Everybody in the whole bloody town knew that we had gotten something to eat but I knew he was building up to something.

'Aye, it was lovely.' Karen answered him, but it was me he was watching in the rear view mirror.

McGroarty began to drive the car slowly, just a few hundred yards, before stopping again and it was far enough to be out of sight of the town. He pulled the car over onto the side of the road, quietly parking it halfway up on the ditch. We slid slightly to the left. This time he switched the engine off.

The Sergeant turned around in his seat as much as he possibly could, puffing and moving sloth-like for he was unable to exert too much energy. I knew he wanted to face us. He rested his elbow on the back of his seat, making the twisting of his body more balanced. He was overbearing, confident and his body odour hung heavy in the air and made me feel light headed.

'Now I know you have been through a lot these last few days, and probably for longer if the truth be told.'

He was doing his best to make his tone sympathetic, make us believe that he somehow cared. 'I don't want to make this any harder on you girls than it already is…but a piece of important information has come my way.'

I looked straight at him, my teeth where clenched and I opened my eyes wider. I wondered what he knew.

'You Adele,' he said holding my stare. 'You were at home all yesterday morning with your Mammy…am I correct in saying that?'

'You are, Sergeant McGroarty.' I answered in a mocking tone.

'Can you tell me at what time approximately it was when you left the house?

I wasn't sure what answer to give.

'I don't know exactly Sergeant, you see Lauren…Mammy wasn't well, she was in bed and I asked her if she needed anything, but she didn't, she just wanted to go to sleep.'

I was aware that I should tell him as little as possible, keep my answers simple, simplicity was easier to recount, and besides I don't think he thought there was much inside my head to begin with.

'Why did you go into the town?'

'I wanted to get some fresh air…like I told you when you were…I was only trying to…there was something that I needed…that's all!' My tone was intolerant and I was unable to finish anything I started to say. Each sentence spiralled into incoherence.

'Right I see…well I was in the post office there and I was talking to Margaret on the switchboard…you know Margaret don't you?'

We both nodded. Everybody knew Margaret and Margaret knew everything about everybody. Her job as the local telephone switchboard operator was very informative. People would swear on the holy bible that they could hear the scribbling of a pencil in the background when you were making a call.

People were relieved that her job was finally being phased out. A lot of complaints had been made about how people could hear her coughing or shuffling about when they were trying to have a private conversation on the telephone.

'Well, Margaret was telling me that your Mammy placed a phone call to a number in Glasgow yesterday morning…now she didn't listen in…but she said she did overheard talk about travel arrangements...now who does your Mammy know that lives in Glasgow?'

Oh, the woman on our party line's the nosiest thing, she picks up her receiver when she knows it's my ring, why don't you mind your own business…

Sergeant McGroarty knew full well who lived in Glasgow; he was just testing us, trying to figure out just how co-operative we really were.

'Ellen lives there...she must have phoned Ellen.' Karen said. She knocked me with her knee as she spoke.

'Mmmmm…I thought that's who it might have been meself.' He said slowly.

'So you see this is what I have had to do…I have had to contact the police over there…because I tried to phone this Ellen one on the number that Margaret had, but low and behold, there was no answer…so the police are waiting outside her house and if your Mammy is there they will see her…and all this commotion will have been a waste of valuable police time…and not just here in Rathford!'

146

Ellen wasn't there! Where could she be? Maybe she was at work or maybe she had gone out to the shops, but I knew Lauren had spoken to her. I had heard them talking. Then I began to doubt whether Lauren had actually spoken to Ellen. I knew that Lauren had been in a state. I knew she was acting crazy and all, but I believed her when she had said that she had spoken to Ellen, and Margaret in the switchboard had overheard but what if it wasn't true?

McGroarty was eyeballing me and he must have read the panic on my face. He looked smug, his lips were white and he knew he had had a small victory. Now he knew for certain that I knew more than I was letting on.

Three policemen and a detective bobby came knocking at the door, weile, weile, walia, three policemen and a detective bobby came knocking at the door, down by the river Salia,

Then I remembered about standing beside the phone box at the river, maybe he knew about that as well, maybe he knew that I had been up to something myself.

Are you the woman that killed the child, weile, weile, walia. Are you the woman that killed the child, down by the river Salia.

Oh God, maybe somebody had overheard what I had said to the bus driver. People would have happily volunteered that kind of information. Professional busy bodies didn't need financial rewards for the satisfaction they got from proving information.

'It was meself that broke the case…had the vital clue…the essential inside info came from my very own lips…'

They tied her hands behind her back, weile, weile, walia, they tied her hands behind her back, down by the river salia!

'Hhhmmm, well, well, well,' he said. 'Now girls, I will leave you back to your house.'

I held my breath tightly. I was afraid to sigh with relief.

'It's important that you tell me everything you know,' he continued. 'Do you hear me…if you remember any little thing…nobody is going to be annoyed with you…but I am here to do right by the law…and I need to make sure that the people of Rathford do the same!'

The Sergeant manoeuvred sluggishly into his driving position and started the car. He revved the engine determinedly as he inched it carefully from the verge and onto the road again and he deliberately drove slowly. Perhaps he thought his snail pace would give me a chance to break my silence, but I didn't know what to think. I had begun to doubt all that Lauren had told me.

'Please let her have spoken to Ellen, please let it be true.'

'Don't be going wandering again,' Sergeant McGroarty added firmly as we jumped out of the car to freedom. 'You never know who is out there and we don't want anything happening to the both of you as well.'

Karen slammed the door shut and we didn't looking back at him. Karen was getting good at closing doors.

The woman they couldn't lock up

'Fuck you in the arse he will! Fuck you in the arse…heeheehee! Sergeant McGroarty thinks you're a dog and he'll fuck you in the arse!' Mad Annie sang the words.

Mad Annie had been hiding in the hedge across the road from the gateway to our house and she had jumped up as Sergeant McGroarty drove off. His words still echoed in my head, for he had left us with an assurance that he would be back soon. He had done his best to sound official. I was relieved to hear the hum of the car dissolve into the distance.

'I hope you end up at the bottom of a twisted multi-car pile-up, Fuckhead.' I had been screaming into myself before Annie interjected.

'Annie what are you doing…come on…come out of there!' Karen beckoned Annie.

Annie's sudden appearance never startled us. Her abrupt arrival was predictable in a contradictory kind of way. You never knew where or when she might pop up but we were used to her emerging from shadows. Annie never scared us. We were well accustomed to her odd ways.

'Oh dear God Annie, what are you on about?' Karen said to her, sounding shocked.

'Chased I was, chased, poor Annie wasn't wanted, and all Annie wanted to do was to go in and see if she could help find your Mammy…but they chased Annie…*whist*…away with you now Annie…*whist*…don't be making a pest of yourself…*whist*….*whist*!'

'Ach Annie, I wouldn't listen to that lot in there, they just think they're better than the rest of us.' Karen said, attempting to humour her.

'Oh, he's a badden, your Daddy is!' Annie looked closely at us, knowing that she could read our reactions.

'A badden, not good to Annie like you girls are. You don't mind Annie speaking the truth…for Annie knows things…Annie hears things that nobody else is supposed to hear!'

'Come on, sit here for a while with us Annie, don't be worrying yourself, we won't chase you.' Again Karen was being kind.

My reaction to what Annie had just said was that I didn't think I could take much more. I wasn't sure if my legs would carry me. Karen was looking at me perplexed.

'Come on, Adele,' she said bemused. 'We'll sit down with Annie for awhile.'

We went inside the gate and sat on a stump of wood, the remains of a beech tree. It was an ancient tree and after a winter of fierce storms it had dangerously started to lean towards the house. There were many times that I wish it had fallen and demolished the whole place and it had taken six men, a chain saw, a bow saw and a hatchet and God knows what else, six days to cut it down. Oh those were the grand days of camaraderie, debate and discussions. The men used to assemble in the shade of the early afternoon each day and work well into the night. Lauren had to cook for them all and Daddy made us leave the kitchen when the food was being served. And on the final day tractors and car boots were piled high with bags of sticks and the air was filled with happy grunts and groans of thanks and praise at a job well done.

It is not for a moment the Spring is unmade to-day.

I used to love it when I walked under the tree and a flurry of wind dropped an unexpected shower of beach nuts unto me.

These were great trees, it was in them from root to stem: When the men with the 'Whoops' and the 'Whoas' have carted the whole of the whispering loveliness away.

'Push me Annie, push me!'

Half the Spring, for me, will have gone with them.

The milkman was the only one who made any use of the tree stump now and he set the milk on it when he was doing his early morning rounds. Except today he had brought the milk right up to the door, delivered it into the kitchen personally.

Annie sat in the middle of us. It was a tight fit, but we managed to sit either side of her, hunching like gargoyle bookends.

Annie wore layers of clothes that were singed and stained with food and soot. There was unidentifiable dirt, grime and filth, but Annie didn't care. It was hard to tell how old she was because she was so unkempt. Roberta used to make a cup of tea for her everyday and she would tell us to always be kind to Annie.

'She's all alone and there's no harm in her.'

One side of Annie's head was completely bald and she had brushed forward a few fine strands onto her forehead like the way an aging man going bald does to pretend to the world and his mother that he isn't. Some of the men teased Annie and called her Yoda. I don't even think Annie knew who Yoda was!

Annie had a habit of twisting her remaining wisps of hair as she spoke, tightening them onto her index finger and yanking at them. It wouldn't be long until she was completely hairless.

Annie knew fine well that she was the town jester, the fool that nobody paid any heed to, unless they wanted to take a hand out of her.

I was glad to see her, for there was a kind of relief that she brought with her and if Annie liked you it was because you were exactly the way you were.

When we had sat down, Annie took Karen and me by the hand. Her hands were warm.

'Girls, don't be listening to what folks are saying...do you hear me now, and don't be on your own with that McGroarty boy...he fucks you in the arse he does.'

Karen seemed embarrassed by Annie's bluntness so she never spoke. My silence was different.

'Awe, he'll say...come here I have a bit of cheese for you...you like cheese don't you...then he'll grab you by the neck and rip your clothes up and sometimes some of the other men help

151

him and they think you don't know who they are because it's dark and you can't see their faces…but Annie knows who they are…don't be on your own girls with the likes of him…Annie knows who they are…they think Annie doesn't know anything about sex…but Annie knows…and Annie knows it's wrong to be fucked in the arse like a dog.'

'We'll stick together don't you worry, Annie.' Karen said as she gave Annie's hand a squeeze to reassure her. I stared straight ahead for I couldn't look at them and if Annie had caught my gaze she would know that I was concealing something.

'Maybe you're Daddy fucked your Mammy in the arse and that's why she went away. Annie wanted to go away but she didn't know how, they put you in the madhouse if you tell, Annie doesn't want to go to the madhouse…they fuck you up the arse in there too!'

I knew Annie couldn't lie, that she was only capable of speaking the truth no matter how crude it sounded.

Karen and I never reacted, we didn't know how to and we didn't know what to say, for we didn't disbelieve her and we didn't tell her to shut up. I felt sorry for her, sorry that in her madness she understood things in a way that nobody else ever would.

'Away with you…clear off!' A voice bellowed behind us as a stone hit Annie sharply on the arm and just missed mine. Annie jumped up, she didn't even turn around to see who it was. She just ran onto the road as fast as she could.

'Away with you…you crazy old witch…we have enough fucking madness in this place.'

I didn't have to look around to see who was shouting or who had thrown the stone at Annie. I knew my Daddy's voice well and I also knew that he always hit what he aimed at.

She knocked him for six

'You two conniving little bitches come here right this minute…we are going to settle this once and for all.'

Daddy was trying to muster up the forces of his wrath to put *the fear of God* into us but really he just looked like some vain actor desperately hoping that he was convincing his audience that he truly felt the emotion that his role demanded.

And Caesar's spirit, raging for revenge, with Ate by his side come hot from hell, Shall in these confines with a monarch's voice. Cry "Havoc!" and let slip the dogs of war.

Daddy hated us talking to Annie and his reaction to her being present was nothing new.

'That wan should have been drowned at birth, a bloody torture she is.'

There was no harm in Annie but I suppose that didn't matter for he hated everything we did or anybody who shown kindness to us.

Mad Annie had scuttled off as fast as she could but I knew she wouldn't get far. Her nose would be bothering her. She would find a good vantage point, a bit of the way down the road. She would sit in some bush or hedge like a clucking hen. Annie was patient when it came to waiting and watching.

Once I saw a little bird come hop, hop, hop. So I cried: 'little bird won't you stop, stop, stop.' I was going to the window, to say: 'how do you do?' when she shook her little wings and far away she flew.

And then like a portent reaching the mind's-eye of the soothsayer the moment shifted and even the light changed. I looked Daddy straight in the eye and saw something ugly had manifest and it's hard to explain for it wasn't tangible and it wasn't a look or a gesture or anything that you could explain with words…but you just felt it in every bone of your knowing.

153

'You two get over here this minute.' Daddy's voice was soft, coaxing almost.

Karen and I didn't move.

'Get over here now…I said get the fuck over here!' This time his command was firm and each word he spoke sprayed saliva from his mouth.

'I'm not going anywhere with you.' I looked at him defiantly and rooted myself to the ground.

'I'm not going anywhere with you ever again, do you hear me…you killed her.'

'I didn't fucking kill her,' he spat maliciously.

'And you seem to be the only one certain that she's dead…how the fuck do you know that she's dead!'

My Daddy calmly strutted a few feet into the garden towards a willow tree and without a sound twisted a branch from it. He began thinning the smaller twigs and scattering them at his feet. He didn't turn around to look at us and we stood in the calm of his preparations.

Daddy then raised his head and directed his gaze toward me while at the same time pulling the stick firmly between his thumb and the index finger of his left hand before finally raising it and whooshing it to cut the air in front of him.

Pearl suddenly came bounding into the yard as if she too felt something had beckoned her to intervene. She didn't get a chance to speak for Daddy turned on her.

'Get you the fuck into that house and don't come out until I tell you…don't let anybody out of that fucking door…they're my wains and I will sort them out…nobody will tell me what to do with my own wains…do you hear me…now fuck off.' His voice rose again with rage and determination.

Pearl left quickly. I don't know if she was afraid of him or she just didn't know what to do, but she turned heel and left us in the yard with him.

Daddy propelled himself forward and in one awkward leap grabbed me and simultaneously swung viciously with the stick. It hissed loudly in the air before it came down curving competently and brutally onto my back. I tried to cower from him, roll myself into a ball, but any attempt at self preservation was futile. He grabbed me by the shoulder and hauled me ferociously over his raised knee. He was balancing on one leg and swooped the stick into the air again, putting all of his strength and anger into the swing that he was about to deliver.

I screamed out in pain even before the stick hit me for the second time. Then I couldn't stop screaming. The sound just kept coming and coming. I was frantic. I couldn't move either. His grip was fixed and he was too strong.

'Did you fuck her in the arse…and that's why she left.' Karen was beside us and it was her voice that stopped him delivering the third blow.

I was now able to move a little and I turned to look at Karen but she was staring at him defiantly. Her teeth were bared and she knew exactly that what she had said would make him turn on her.

'What did you say?' his voice was shocked and high pitched. I had never seen him open-mouthed before but it was only momentarily because he threw me violently to the ground and reached to grab Karen. He shouted at her again as he tried to shake the life out of her.

'What the fuck did you say to me!' Karen was completely limp in his arms and he twisted her easily as he raised the stick high in the air and brought it down on her with such fierceness that it broke in two.

'Did you fuck her in the arse?' I said it this time.

But before my Daddy could do anything else, someone was beside us and punched him viciously in the face. The slap was delivered with such strength that I think we all felt it. The noise resounded in the air like a shot from a gun that is set to scare away crows. Daddy wobbled in slow motion and fell over.

155

'You will never lay a finger on these girls again…do you hear me you piece of fucking shit…you fucking bastard…!'

I got up off the ground to see who it was. It was Ellen, it had to be Ellen. Then I fell down again and wailed, wailed like Monica, except I wasn't pretending.

My Daddy stumbled to his feet.

'What kind of animal beats his own children?' Ellen shouted at him in disgust. She wasn't one inch afraid of him.

'Is she with you?' Daddy snorted at her through gritted teeth.

'Is she fucking with you, you lesbian bitch!' He growled as he staggered, trying to recover from the blow.

'I don't know where she is…but I do know that if you lay another finger on these wains…no threat in the land will keep me away…do you hear me…you piece of fucking shit…no fucking threat in the land!'

I had never seen my Daddy cower in my entire life. Not until that moment.

A place called 'safe'

Ellen had safely locked us in her car before walking back towards the house. Her step was firm and confident and I was glad that the car doors were locked and I wasn't going to open them for anyone. I was hunched in the back seat and was rocking back and forth and had my knees tucked under my chin. I felt stressed and relieved at the same time and the contradictory combination of the emotions was causing the momentum. Karen was looking at me afraid. I couldn't stop shaking. I felt as if my heart would stop beating if I stopped rocking. It was the only thing keeping it alive.

Believe me if all those endearing young charms, which I gaze on so fondly today...

It was strange to be able to look at the house from the safety of the car. I didn't have to face anymore interrogations.

'Please God, please God, don't let Ellen leave our side!'

Were to change by tomorrow, And fleet in my arms, Like fairy gifts fading away...

This was truly unbelievable. Someone had come who could stand up to Daddy. I didn't want to take my eyes of Ellen. If I looked away she might disappear and my head would break if she disappeared.

Though would'st still be adored, As this moment thou art, Let thy loveliness fade as it will, And around the dear ruin, Each wish of my heart, Would entwine itself, Verdantly still.

'It's okay Adele...it's okay...he's gone.'

Karen was beside me in the back seat and she was trying to wrap me in her arms so I would calm down and I must have been frightening her. Waves of emotion were rushing through my body. I could feel beads of sweat on my brow yet I felt cold. Tears kept running down my face.

'Sshh Adele...sshh!'

Pearl had come out to the front door and was talking to Ellen. Pearl had her arms folded staunchly under her proud breasts, her chest was raised high in the air. Ellen looked much more comfortable in her body. She was rooted to the doorstep and no-one was going to sidestep her. There was a bit of gesticulation going on between her and Pearl and it really didn't look like anything that Ellen couldn't handle for she stood steadfast.

Daddy had disappeared somewhere and I still expected him to reappear at any second.

'Please hurry up Ellen, please.'

Monica emerged like Pearl's shadow into the gloom of the doorframe and was trying to join in on the debate, but her attempt looked half-hearted as usual. We knew they were objecting to us going with Ellen.

'You're no blood relation and you have no right interfering! Those girls have been through enough and they don't need you confusing them even more!'

You didn't need to be able to lip read to know the kind of thing they would be saying.

Ellen suddenly threw both her hands into the air and walked away, leaving a bewildered Monica and Pearl dumbstruck, an expression that perfectly suited their faces.

'I'm here because your Mammy wanted my help,' she said to us in the car as we drove into town. I had settled down a bit, although I was still huddled into myself, but I was feeling much better because Ellen was in the car with us.

'I have always respected what she wanted, even though that was tough at times. I won't be telling you girls what to do, but you know I'm afraid that he'll kill you if he gets his hands on you. And I don't think he'll be best pleased with me either. But I will not be bullied by him and I promise I'll do everything I can to keep you safe.'

Her promise rose up in me and gave me a euphoric surge of hope,

Hallelujah, hallelujah, hallelujah, hallelujah hal-le-lu-jah...

It was as if a magician had shaken his cloak and released a flock of white birds into the sky. Nobody had ever made me a promise like that before. I had never known that a place called 'safe' existed.

'I promise I'll do everything I can to keep you safe.'

The words pulsed to the rhythm of my thumping heartbeat.

'I promise...keep you safe...everything I can...'

The echo soothed and calmed me each time I intoned her affirmation. I liked the hint of the Scottish accent in her voice and I wanted her to keep talking.

Queen of the purple rinse brigade

Upon her arrival in Rathford, Ellen had decided to book a room in the Drummond Arms for it was Rathford's only hotel, and although there were a few B&B's in the town she thought that there might be a chance of a bit more privacy in the hotel.

The Drummond Arms was tall and looming and overlooked the river. The main structure had been grotesquely extended by a series of contorted mishmash shapes that were added on, as and when required, without any aesthetic considerations. A splattering of Georgian windows offered a variety of gaping criss-crossed rectangles from which to scrutinize the vista. An excessive number of blue doorways provided a multitude of entrance points and could easily confuse the uninitiated, so you usually went for the noisiest one. The exterior had at one time been whitewashed but was now shoddy and stained and looked sad and dilapidated.

MINOR DRAMATIS PERSONAE
DOREEN, hotel owner, town trend setter, hostess aficionado, Queen of the Purple rinse Brigade.
DON, Doreen's husband, a shadow of his former self, the quiet man who lives for a quiet life.

Doreen and Don, the proprietors, had inherited the hotel from Doreen's parents and in the forties and fifties the hotel had a good reputation, far and wide, buzzing with holidaymakers and catering occasionally for a wedding and the odd honeymooning couple. They were especially busy at bank holiday weekends.

Doreen had been an only child and her parents had doted on her and she didn't have to learn how to do anything for herself. By the time the hotel was in her hands she seemed to think that it would just run all by itself.

Doreen and Don never had any children of their own and they regularly affirmed that it never really bothered them. Doreen said that the lack of responsibility gave them the independence to run the hotel, owning your own business took up a lot of your time and she had standards to maintain.

Doreen's high standards only seemed to apply to her personal presentation for she was always well groomed. She had her hair set once a week and a purple rinse added and was never seen without make-up. Her clothes and shoes and jewellery always matched. So whatever she wore, on any given day, was co-ordinated. She had a blue outfit, a green outfit and a beige outfit.

'One to suit every mood.' She would say as she tossed her head back, feigning nonchalance. Don was more of a background figure, for Doreen although she would never have been seen dead in a pair of trousers, gave the orders and determined the lay of the land.

Doreen's perpetual habit of whispering asides to the guests gave the impression that she was discreet and trustworthy when it came to catering for her guest's requirements but her values weren't really noticeable in a building that had fallen into rack and ruin. Paint peeled and flecked from the interior walls, the patterns in the carpets were threadbare and indistinguishable. The place hadn't been up-dated in decades.

Doreen had been delighted to see Ellen. She had given her a great welcome, but not enough to hug her. Ellen might have a quick grope or something. 'Slip the hand' as they say. Everyone in the town knew that Joseph had to chase Ellen as she was always trying it on with his wife. Doreen had shuddered at the thought. She would lock her room door at night. Don wouldn't be much protection if the likes of her decided to have a go at you but having Ellen stay with her was a coup indeed and it was well worth the risk.

Doreen had quickly updated Ellen on the current drama and she didn't need to ask one question at all. Doreen thought that maybe Ellen would reciprocate and tell her all that she knew also but she had only asked to be shown to her room.

Ellen had sat in the room for a couple of hours, looking out the window, floundering in her own memories of the town, watching the swans moving slowly and gracefully on the river, contemplating their own reflection. She was desperately trying to gather the courage to come out to our little house of horrors.

The hotel bar had filled with people as the news of Ellen's arrival spread. Don had to phone for extra staff to come in, they hadn't been that busy since 'Wee Tommy' and his rockin rolling show band had played there in 1978. They had got 'Wee Tommy' cheap too, his mother and father had spent their honeymoon in the hotel and he had always wanted to bring them back. People still talked about the great night that was had. The Drummond Arms hotel was the place to be then and the place to be today of all days.

Three gals holed up in the Drummond Arms

When we arrived at the Hotel, Doreen insisted on walking us to the room. Ellen had assured her that we knew where to find it, after all she had been in the room earlier in the day, but Doreen was adamant and she could hardly contain herself with excitement.

'So girls, any more news on your Mammy? She has caused quite a stir indeed.' Doreen was doing most of the talking as we manoeuvred up the two narrow rickety flights of stairs that seemed more like a slope with no steps. It was quite a nervous climb towards a destination that seemed to lead us away from solid ground. The carpet far from being comforting seemed to shift occasionally as if one might fall and plummet downwards again.

'Nothing more than you were able to tell me this morning yourself.' Ellen said back to her.

'Now if youse need anything at all…and I mean anything, give me a shout, I'll be at the other end of that phone ready and waiting.' Then Doreen paused outside the room door, looked around furtively to make sure no one overheard her and whispered. 'It's an internal line, to the switchboard here in the hotel, so nobody else will listen in on anything you say!'

'Thank you Doreen…you've been very kind.' It was easy to tell that there was no conviction in Ellen's voice. Ellen looked impatiently as if she wished that Doreen would vanish into thin air.

We entered the room, it was getting dark outside and Ellen switched on a small bedside lamp. The shade was crooked and transparent and it was hard not to stare at the glare of the light bulb.

Karen and me wearily sat on the edge of one of the single beds. It was obvious we were awkward and felt out of place. I never thought I would ever see the inside of a hotel room. They were places either for people in country and western songs that had doomed love affairs or places for rich people, people of a certain standing and I was well aware of the fact that I was neither and didn't belong. There was no novelty in the surroundings, just unease.

'I think we will get you two cleaned up first, you look like you have been living in the wilds for months.' Ellen shook her head in pity as she spoke.

I went into the bathroom to take a shower first, we only had a bath at home and the only other showers I had ever used were the ones at school, which didn't really look like much, and the water was always cold, so you only stayed in them for as little time as possible. The Nuns didn't like you to loiter anyway.

'Come along now girls, chop, chop.' Sister Geraldine would say quickly, puffing out her fleshy throat like a toad.

Sister Geraldine was the only one who loitered in the changing rooms and she was even allowed to walk right into the boys shower.

The shower in the hotel seemed really posh and I was frightened to use it. But Ellen switched it on and fiddled confidently with the settings, letting the water splash on the palm of her hand for a few seconds before leaving me alone in the pokey vault. The walls felt like they were made of cardboard and were covered with white woodchip paper and there was a long mirror on one of the walls and I was startled when I saw my naked reflection in it. My upper thighs were covered with bruises and red blotches that made them look like I had been scalded by boiling water and I had rough scratch marks across my stomach and back. The room began to fill with steam and fog the mirror and I was relieved to see my reflection disappear.

Steal away, lets steal away, no reason left to stay, for me and you, let's start anew and darlin' steal away...

I washed quickly; I didn't want to touch any part of my body. I just let the water run over me until my skin and hair were soaked through. I turned the shower off and just stood dripping wet. I felt like I needed somebody to tell me what to do next.

Let's steal away, and chase our dreams and hope they'll never find us, the weary days, the empty nights, we'll leave them all behind us...

164

I pulled on a T-shirt that Ellen had given me. It was too big and it clung graceless to the wetness of my skin and made me feel self-conscious again.

Karen went into the bathroom after I came out.

I sat on the edge of the bed and watched my feet as I scrunched my toes into the carpet.

'Let me check your back,' Ellen said.

'No it's alright.' I replied and flinched slightly and then cringed hoping that Ellen didn't think that I thought she would hurt me.

'I'm okay,' I said. 'It's really Karen that we should be worrying about.'

Ellen looked at me sadly.

I wanted to curl up and go to sleep. My eyelids felt heavy and weary and I longed to rest them.

Poppies... Poppies. Poppies will put them to sleep. Sleeeeep. Now they'll sleeeeep!

'Where is she, Adele?'

Ellen's voice made me jerk out of the semi-slumber that was creeping and reaching its tendrils into me. Her tone was soft and tender and soothing. It was somewhere far away in the ether and I didn't feel like I needed to answer it. I just wanted to keep my eyes shut and let it's vibration continue to calm and comfort me.

'We need to find her.'

'I...I can't remember...really I can't.' And as I answered I slowly crawled up onto the bed. I was so drowsy and what I said was true. I didn't know where to find her. I didn't know anything anymore.

'One more thing,' she had said to me, 'one more thing.' But I really couldn't remember what it was.

Karen came out of the bathroom and Ellen asked her if she wanted her to put a dressing on her cut. Karen nodded and turned her back to us and shyly pulled up her top. There was a raw scourge mark like a raised dirt track from her shoulder blade down to the

165

base of her spine. The flesh was broken in parts. It must have stung like hell and Karen winced quietly as Ellen put some cream on it and then gently covered it with a make-shift bandage.

Karen perched herself onto the other single beds and she sat cross-legged, her back carefully positioned against the padded headboard. The beds jutted out from the wall parallel to each other and were draped with pink candlewick bedspreads that had little bits of the pattern missing, probably picked out by some bored, sleepless guest.

A wardrobe precariously stood in the room; it was painted white and smelt musty. The floor sloped slightly so that the door kept swinging open when you tried to close it. Ellen had pushed her luggage against it to keep it shut.

I remembered the money that Lauren had given to me and I retrieved it from my skirt pocket and showed it to Ellen. I spread it out proudly at my feet, Roberta's bingo winnings 'the little something' she gave to Lauren each time she won.

Ellen was silent. Her soft face was round and resolute and pretty. She was broad, maybe a bit over weight but not in any kind of way that you would worry about. It was just more the way her shape was. She wore a pair of faded jeans and had a flowery blouse tucked inside the waistband. Her hair was brown and cut into a bob. It looked a bit tossed, uneven, but it suited her for she had naturalness about her, a presence that was gentle and reassuring.

Sometimes the way Daddy talked about Ellen it would make you think that she was ugly, but she wasn't, and maybe that is why he was so mad at her. He didn't like the idea that a woman could be smart and pretty and didn't need a man to tell her what to do. There had been a lot of talk when Ellen had sold her mother's farm. You knew that the men didn't like it when a woman made money from the land.

'Who does thon think she is selling that land to some stranger, the local farmers should have a right to the first pickings. She's just putting her two fingers up to the lot of us…smug bitch!'

166

The hotel room felt like a little sanctuary. I imagined we were hiding out in the bell tower of a church. Ellen, Karen and me holed up like bank robbers, counting our loot. I was just starting to relax when the phone gave a shrill ring, making us all jump, even Ellen.

Ellen let it shriek a couple of times before she answered it.

'Okay, send him up.' she said.

'The Sergeant wants to speak to us.' She said as she put the receiver back in place and looked from me to Karen then back to me again.

My head was shaking involuntarily.

'I don't want to see him,' I said. 'I don't want McGroarty or Daddy anywhere near us...you have to make them go away!' I knew my objections were scaring Ellen.

'It's okay Adele, I will stand by whatever you girls want to tell him...do you understand me...but we need to be together on what we tell him.' She began to chew the corner of her thumbnail.

We could hear his footsteps in the hallway outside, and then there was a firm knock at the door...one solid tap...we knew it was McGroarty.

'One minute,' Ellen called. 'The girls are just getting sorted.'

Ellen quickly lifted the money and crumpled it into the drawer of a bedside locker.

'Now girls...we can't contradict anything any of us say.' She whispered quickly. 'If we need to stretch the truth for awhile then we stick together on it and follow my lead if you're stuck for something to say...okay?'

'Okay.' Karen and myself answered in unison. But I wasn't at all reassured.

Ellen opened the door wide and smiled broadly as Sergeant McGroarty strode into the room, he didn't wait to be invited.

'Now girls...don't you look a whole lot better.' He said in his usual condescending tone as he looked around the room.

'Mmm...a whole lot better.' He looked us up and down.

'And it's been a long time since we saw your good self!' McGroarty spoke in a mock sing-song voice as he squared up to Ellen.

Ellen didn't grant him a reply nor did she flinch or alter her stance...he averted his gaze from her.

'Now, now, now, we are all here for the same reason...and that is to get Mammy home safe for these poor girls...wouldn't you agree.'

It was easy to know that Sergeant McGroarty didn't like Ellen. He knew she would stand up to him if he challenged her. As far as he was concerned she was one of those lesbian types with a mind that couldn't be changed by any man. But this was his town, his jurisdiction up to the parish boundary and he wouldn't have anybody show up and try to undermine his authority, especially a woman, who didn't even want to be a woman.

'So, she phoned you yesterday morning...that much we can all agree on.' McGroarty was looking at me again. He couldn't hold eye contact with Ellen for very long and it was my turn to feel smug.

'That's right,' Ellen said. 'And when she didn't get off the bus last night I was worried and decided to come here myself instead.'

'Worried you say? What did she say that would make you worry now?' This time he looked at Ellen and boldly held her eye.

'She said that Joseph had beaten her badly and she was afraid for her life and she said she needed to get away from him before he did something terrible to her.'

Her directness made the Sergeant visibly uneasy, he put his hand into his pockets and rattled his keys.

'Well, I suppose that would make anybody worry.'

'So can you tell us where else you have looked for her Sergeant?' Ellen had decided that questioning him would give her the upper hand. But he knew this.

168

'Mmm' he said. 'I think we may have exhausted all possibilities at this stage. We were hoping that you could give us some fresh information.'

'Well as you can see…I've not long arrived myself and I am trying to get a handle on the situation. Now I believe you have already questioned the girls and as well you know they could do with a rest…so if you don't mind…'

'Oh I don't mind at all.' Sergeant McGroarty was frustrated and he knew he wasn't going to get any more help out of us but then he also knew he hadn't got any to start with either.

'No I don't mind…but mind you don't take these girls anywhere…you're not their legal guardian, and if you take them out of my jurisdiction we will have to look at the situation as one of kidnapping…and we don't want to make matters more complicated. So my advice is that your best bet is to let us know of your movements while you are in town.' He sounded like some awful sheriff, letting the outlaws know who was boss,

I'm the sheriff around these parts ma'am, this tin star gives me authority and you won't be leavin' town unless I kick you out!

Yes, sir deputy Dawg!

'Why would I be taking the girls anywhere?' Ellen answered him frowning to indicate that he had said something stupid and then she continued. 'But I will pay heed to your advice…and can you also keep us informed of any developments…thank you…for as you said yourself…we are all worried.'

As Ellen finished her sentence she put her hand on the door to signify that she expected him to leave.

The Sergeant was about to obey but he changed his mind.

'One more thing, Ellen,' he said. 'There's folk in this town that are not too happy about you sharing a room with these innocent young girls, with the way you are and all…so my advice is that if you are all staying the night here in the Drummond Arms…then you rent another room for yourself.'

169

Ellen closed the door in his face, but we knew he was happy with this victory. He had succeeded in riling her.

Goodnight Irene, I'll see you in my dreams

I picked a dandelion clock, And I held it near my nose, I blew the pretty fluff away, And counted up my blows.

I had been asleep for a couple of hours and I must have been tossing and turning for I could see her in my dream, she held a dandelion clock in her outstretched hand and was beckoning me to take it. Her skin was translucent and there was blood dripping from her wrists, dripping like the water from the spout at the side of the house. I skipped towards her chanting in a child's sing-song voice.

"It's one o'clock, it's two o'clock," I gave a great big puff – "It's three o'clock, it's four o'clock." Away went all the fluff. My dandelion clock was right, for mother called to me, "Come in and wash your grubby hands, It's nearly time for tea."

The winged seeds from the dandelion began to flutter and disperse and I tried to catch them and she moved deeper into the forest until I could only hear her whisper.

'One more thing,' she kept saying over and over again, 'just one more thing.'

I jumped startled out of my sleep. It took me a few seconds to realise where I was.

Ellen was sitting on the edge of the bed.

'You're safe' she said. 'You're okay…you're okay, it's me, Ellen…ssshhh…'

Ellen held me close and rocked softly with the motion of my body.

'Look Adele…I think it's time we talked, now I don't want to be pressurising you or anything but we need to figure this out.'

Karen was still fast asleep in the other bed. I was groggy but I rubbed my face and tried to wake up. But I needed to keep her out of my head for I didn't need to remember anything bad now that I was safe.

'I know you don't know me,' Ellen said softly, 'but I promise you, you can trust me and I wish there was a way I could make all of this stop. I wish I could have done more to help you before things came to this, but we need to find her first and lay her to rest. I know that she's not in this world anymore…and you're the only one that can find her Adele...we need to find her body before we can do anything else, we owe her that much.'

'How do you know she's not here anymore?' I asked.

'I just do, Adele. I just know.'

Ellen didn't need to say anything that would persuade me to trust her, I just knew I could, for there was no fog around her.

'I remember what it was…the one more thing…I remember now…she asked me to help her with one more thing.' I looked sadly at Ellen. I wished that she could read my mind but she couldn't so instead I pointed at Karen and said.

'She thinks that Lauren didn't care about her. But Lauren was confused and she couldn't remember about any of the rest of them…she just thought it was only me.'

'Only you what?' Ellen asked.

'She didn't know that she had more wains, every time I said their names she didn't remember, she wouldn't speak about them. I think if she had,' I hesitated then added. 'She couldn't have done what she did…oh dear god…she had to pretend that they weren't there.'

'What did she want you to do Adele? You said you remembered. If you don't tell me I can't help you…it's important that I know.'

Ellen brushed my hair away from my face, just the way Lauren had that last morning at the kitchen table and then I was suddenly overwhelmed and I couldn't hide it inside me anymore for it reminded me of Lauren and I looked at Ellen.

'A rope…oh Jesus…she asked me to go to the shed and get her a rope…oh Jesus…I went out to the shed and I got her the rope!'

Do as you're told

Oh the dead wood stage is coming on over the hill…!

I am standing outside the shed and it is in our backyard and it is a small, unplastered, crude breezeblock building.

Where the Injun arrows are thicker than porcupine quills…

The walls are draughty and cold. The building stands beside the outside toilet/coal house and Daddy keeps his tools in it and bits of broken instruments and workman stuff.

Dangerous land! No time to delay!

We're not allowed to go into it but I must have because I have the rope in my hands. The rope feels thick and strong and hairy. It feels like a horse's tail.

So, Whip crack-away! Whip crack-away! Whip crack-away!

Daddy uses the rope for towing things with his tractor. When some neighbour's car breaks down or gets bogged in a field or something.

Whip crack-away! Whip crack-away! Whip crack-away!

I know why I am bringing it to her. I know exactly why she wants it. I am still in my nightdress and my legs are blue with the cold and I am trembling uncontrollably and the little blond hairs on my legs and arms stand on edge. I am covered with goose bumps and my skin looks like a plucked chicken.

Whip crack-away! Whip crack…whip crack…

I couldn't believe that I had it in my hands and that I was going to walk back into the kitchen and give it to her. But I do and I can't say that I walked fast or slow or anything. I just walk back into the house with it lying across my hands, like the way rings are presented on a cushion at a wedding. She takes it from me and she thanks me. She says thanks!

'Go and get dressed now,' she says. 'And when you come back down stairs I won't be here but you know what you have to do. Promise me now that you won't marry him and that you will get on that bus.'

173

'I promise,' I said. And I didn't really know what I was saying for I just wanted to stand and look at her for I knew that if I stopped looking at her I would never see her ever again.

'Go on now, do as you're told.' She spoke as if she had asked me to do some chore, like any old run-of-the-mill request that she had made on any given day in our lives.

I went up the stairs and got dressed slowly and I don't know how long it took me and when I came back down she was gone. That's how she said I should remember. I would come back down the stairs and she would be gone.

I knew where to find her

I was in Ellen's arms sobbing and shaking wildly. I remember thinking that I must have looked like mad Annie or maybe mad Annie wouldn't look so mad if she was in the room with me at that moment. Ellen was doing her best to sooth me.

'It's alright,' she said over and over while repeatedly stroking my hair. 'It's all right.'

But it wasn't alright, it wasn't alright. There was nothing alright about what I had done. Now I knew why Lauren had wanted me to go, she wanted me to go because I had helped her. I had been her accomplice and she knew what would happen to me if anyone ever found out. The truth of what had happened was far worse than any story I could ever make up in my head.

Karen awoke.

'What's wrong?' she asked groggily.

'Everything is just catching up with her...now don't you worry...we'll figure this out.'

'Nobody needs to know,' Ellen whispered reassuringly to me as Karen got out of bed and cuddled into me as well.

'We need to find her.' Ellen was chewing her thumb nail again.

'We need to find her and get as far away from here as we can, you're not safe here, Adele!'

How could she say 'not safe', I believed that I was safe! I couldn't think that I wasn't safe and my head hurt and I couldn't get the fog to clear and the panic was mixing me up again and...

'Right,' Ellen said decisively, this is what we are going to do...let's all have a good think...together we can figure this out...where do we think she could have went?'

Karen looked at me blankly.

'Let start with somewhere straightforward...mmm...where was her favourite place?' Ellen asked.

'She loved the Lough.' Karen said. 'Up Mooney's lane, she used to go for walks up there…but we were there today…'

'She's not anywhere where there is water.' I said with irritation.

'But how do you know that?' Karen asked.

'It's alright Karen.' Ellen interrupted. 'If Adele doesn't think she's near water then let's just go with that.'

'I just know Karen,' I said. 'I just know.'

I was glad Ellen had backed me up. I didn't want to tell her how I knew.

'She spoke about a boy…some boy she knew before she met Daddy.'

'Oh I know who that was.' Ellen said and smiled sadly. His name was Mark Deeney, she was mad about him...and he was so handsome, and he was mad about her as well…they were inseparable that summer before…and I used to help them arrange places to meet and I don't know what happened…he had to leave with his parents and he said he'd come back and he never did…his parents were well off…they had moved here from Galway…very well educated people…maybe they thought she wasn't good enough.'

The sky was clear, the morning fair, not a breath came over the sea, when Mary left her highland home and wandered forth with me…

Then I knew, in that moment. I knew where to find her.

Ready or not here I come

'I know where she is, I know where to find her.'

I kept saying it over and over again. I was wildly excited, like I had worked out a puzzle that had tortured my head for days and your attention shifts momentarily and the answer was right in front of you the entire time.

I began to get dressed quickly and Karen and Ellen were trying to do the same but I hadn't time to wait on them. The location was clear in my head and I was so certain and I left the room and ran down the stairs and bolted from the hotel. I felt light, like the breeze was carrying me to her, *ar nós na gaoithe*.

'Lauren, Lauren I know where to find you, I know where you are. Ready or not here I come!'

Ellen and Karen were running after me. Sergeant McGroarty had waited outside the hotel all night and some of the other men were with him and they followed also, but I didn't care. I didn't care who knew where I was going or why, I just kept running.

I could hear Karen shouting behind me, 'Where are you going? Where are you going? Adele, please!'

But I couldn't answer her. Everything was so vivid and I thought if I was distracted for a second, then I would forget again, the fog would come back and I wouldn't be able to see her.

I remembered she had told me about the place in the woods that she would go to meet Mark Deeney. The forest was near our house and it was government owned and had been planted and replanted over the years with invasive conifers. Trees that had left the land parched and were planted so close together that nothing else could grow. There was only one native tree in the thicket, a tall brave sycamore that stood beside the skeletal remains of an old stone farmhouse. It had been their favourite meeting place. They would sit on the moss covered walls and talk and make their childish plans. I knew exactly where it was because I had played there often myself, and yet I was unaware that it could tell the story of Lauren's first love.

By far the sweetest flower there, was the Rose of Allendale…

I tried to imagine how she had managed to climb the tree and fix the rope onto it, but I couldn't think, I couldn't allow my mind to see that moment and all I could see was a pool of blood on the ground beneath her and blood stains on her legs. Her head hung to the side and her neck looked like it was broken, her tongue stuck out swollen from her mouth.

That would be the last image I would have of Lauren. I had wanted to see her one more time.

Post-mortem photography

It had taken two days from her disappearance before Lauren's body was found...she had gone into some nearby woods and hung herself...her faded blue, cheap polyester nightdress transparent on her sallow skin...her pitiful little body suspended limp and abandoned. Ending her own life was the first decision she had made in years.

The trees were still and the smell of rotting pine needles filled the morning air. A soft haze shrouded the scene. Dull shafts of light struck smoky and solemn and spear-like through gaps in the trees. Everything seemed stationary...time...movement...sound ...like a ghostly snapshot...and then having to walk into it...having to move forward and become part of the photograph...I began to shake and I don't know whether it was from cold or fear or lack of sleep...or shock...but that was it, it was over and I had found her...I tried to move forward but I couldn't...maybe I shouted...I know there was a sound, but I am not sure if it came from me.

Keenin' on the back road

Lauren and I had spent her last few hours on the planet together and she made me promise that I would leave and get away in a way that she couldn't. Those last few hours that morning were to be the first and only time that my mother confided in me.

'Why had I helped her? Why had I been so stupid? She was the last person in all of this mess that should have died!'

I had been carried out of the forest and I don't know who carried me or how much time had passed but I was sitting in the back of an ambulance and it was white and had a red stripe on both sides and a blue light revolved silently on the roof. The back doors were wide opened and I was perched on the top step. Two paramedics were examining me. A pink blanket was draped around my shoulders and they kept asking me my name, asking me what day of the week it was or something stupid like that. The kind of questions that I had asked Lauren the morning I found her on the kitchen floor, the same ones she couldn't answer.

People had been told to move back from the scene and a team of experts had been called in and Sergeant McGroarty was striding about impatiently checking his wrist watch and waiting on them. A number of Gardaí from local districts had arrived and they stood like a row of blue fence posts and were asserting command of the area. They had marked a boundary around the site with blue and white tape. Some people had to be pushed forcefully out of the woods and the edge of the road was lined with a lot of people and among the flurry was a photographer and he was followed by a fidgety journalist with a pen who was asking questions and jotting down people's replies really quickly, without even looking at what he was writing in his notebook. He wore a press badge pinned to the top pocket of his crumpled jacket.

Karen and Ellen were coming towards me and I couldn't lift my head to look at them. I didn't want them to see me. I didn't want to have to look anyone in the face ever again. Ellen knew what I had done. Maybe she had told McGroarty or maybe she had told Karen and everyone was going to hate me and maybe they would put me in a dungeon and lock me up and throw away the key. I was the only one that could have stopped her. But instead I had done a terrible thing.

'Oh Jesus, I'm sorry Ellen, I'm so sorry…what have I done?'

Ellen was beside me hurriedly and she told me firmly to be quiet.

'None of this is your fault…now don't be saying anything…promise me you won't say anything to anyone. I will try to get you back to the hotel in a minute but you'll have to be quiet. Not another word.'

'Karen,' Ellen said, 'now stay here with your sister and don't go anywhere with anyone, do you hear me, no matter what anyone says or tells you to do, stay right here until I come back. I'm going to see if I can take you girls back to the hotel, there's nothing more we can do here.'

Ellen touched my shoulder gently before turning and dissolving into the crowd again. I didn't want her to leave. I needed her to be near me.

Karen must have read my thoughts for she whispered.

'Ellen won't be long, don't worry.'

Karen's voice was choked and I could feel her confusion and everything felt sunken like a moment of unmitigating defeat after having put so much heart into trying to achieve something.

'What are we going to do, Karen?' I asked. 'I don't ever want to see him again!'

Then we were quiet, for what can you say? How can you know how your life will be in the next second or minute or hour when something like this happens?

We sat despondent beside each other, our feet dangling above the ground, it felt like we were sitting on the edge of a pier and it was regatta day. We watched the commotion closely, our eyes absorbing the bustle of people's reactions, absorbing a scene that

181

didn't need us anymore and we could be delegated to the periphery of all that was going on.

Nobody came near us, for whatever reasons, people just gazed at us from a distance. I didn't really care. I didn't care whether they felt shame or sorrow or that they just didn't know what to say to us. Even mad Annie eyed us from a distance. I didn't want anyone near me, except for Karen and Ellen.

Everything seemed chaotic; more people arrived, mostly on foot and some on bicycles and they dismounted casually as they freewheeled their bikes stealthily to a firm stop and then leaned them securely against the ditch. Caps were tipped humbly and heads shook at each other in disbelief. People spoke very little and stopped in the middle of what they were trying to utter.

There was no more room along the roadside for cars to park. Then, I could see Ellen again and I was so relieved and then I could hear Monica crying, her wailing rising above everyone and everything and then I could hear more people crying…why were so many people crying?

One night only

The next few days moved as if I was trying to propel myself
unsuccessfully through zero gravity…I can remember waiting for
something, just waiting and I had to strain to even hear a sound for
everything was muffled and the world had been gagged into
submission and life was unmoving like Lauren's body suspended in
the woods. The panic that I felt had subsided and the confusion was
gone.

    *Ninety years without slumbering, tick, tock, tick, tick, It's life
seconds numbering, tick tock, tick, tock, And it stopped short, never
to go again, when the old man died.*

    Time had finally stood still.

    Lauren's remains had been cut down from the tree and
removed from the woods under a Garda presence. Her body was
taken from the scene for a post-mortem by State pathologist and I
didn't want to think about her being passed around by so many
hands like a *pass the parcel* party game or a procession of Stoats
who carry their dead with regal solemnity. Rumours of an inquest
were wildly inaccurate. There was no evidence of any struggle or
other assistance in the ending of her life. The coroner's report clearly
stated cause of death was suicide by hanging in the case of Lauren
Doherty. Time of death seemed officially certain between 9.30 am
and 10.30 am on 08/01/1987. McGroarty's left-handed signature,
bold and slant across the documentation cleanly established his
investigation. In the woods he had found nothing suspicious. At
Lauren's place of residence there had been a rapid disposal of
Valium and Lorazepam capsules just like two half packets of tic tac
from the bathroom cabinet down the lavatory.

    Her death was listed under 'sudden and unexpected' and
even though the cause was known, and blatantly obvious, they still
had to rule out foul play. It was the way things had to be done
legally. People needed to know exactly how she had died even
though nobody gave a damn about how she had lived. Her death

certificate, issued by the coroner concurred with all official findings and the matter was closed.

We stayed in the hotel with Ellen. Doreen updated us whenever she heard anything new. Even Doreen felt sorry for us. She carried food up to our room and cried as she left.

'God bless you girls,' she would say with a lump in her throat. 'Anything you need…anything at all.' I think she actually meant it.

A couple of days past and Sergeant McGroarty visited us in the hotel room.

'Your Mammy,' he said and then he cleared his throat. 'Lauren Doherty's remains were brought to the marital home at 6 o'clock this evening.' He made the announcement in his best official matter of fact tone, 'The cause of death had been determined and there was no need to question anyone further.'

Not one of us made any comment and we all just stared at him and McGroarty suddenly seemed somewhat bewildered…it was strange to see him like that and the more we stared the more awkward he became and you knew the last thing he wanted was to have to be in our company.

'Your Daddy has said that you can go out to the house…for the wake that is…he feels you should be there so to speak.' He added reluctantly.

McGroarty looked up at the ceiling and kinda whistled between his teeth.

'Right then…right then…I'll show myself out.'

The journey to the house felt different and it wasn't an easy one to make and some part of me knew that it would be the last time that I would ever have to make it.

Lauren's coffin was closed. Her body was so badly discoloured and swollen that it would have been wrong to make people look at her. Well, at least, that's what Pearl said when we got out to the house. She mumbled some incoherent explanation in a disturbed whisper, using bizarre hand gestures.

Will you walk into my parlour? Said the spider to the fly, 'tis the prettiest little parlour that you ever did spy...

As we stepped over the threshold people willingly parted to let us through and stood awkwardly back from us.

The way into the parlour is up a winding stair, and I've a many curious thing to shew when you are there...

The mood in the house was heavy and the air was thick with the smell of stewed tea.

'Oh, no, no,' said the little fly, 'to ask me is in vain, for who goes up your winding stair can ne'er come down again.'

Our every move was scrutinised for our reactions, more than anybody else's ours were crucial to the undertone of the event.

There were trays with little delicately floral patterned china cups and saucers sitting on the kitchen table. I had never seen them before. Paper doilies adorned plates; cake stands were heaped with little delicate homemade buns and boxes of biscuits as well as dishes lined with cigarettes that occupied any available space. The fragrance of coconut cream biscuits drifted past every now and again and reminded me of scented night stock.

There were a lot of women shuffling in the kitchen, rattling cutlery, cracking hardboiled eggs against the sink, buttering bread like robots and putting tea into gleaming stainless steel pots. The tea was then tested by pouring the tiniest gloop into the gleaming sink and this was followed by a nod of approval or disapproval.

As we passed into the living room the people sitting on the rows of chairs leaned forward humbly and the people standing leaned back meekly. There was a queue of mourners stretching out the front door and into the yard; people from far and wide had come to pay their respects.

Daddy had insisted that Lauren's remains should be waked for only the one night. The funeral had been delayed long enough with all the procedures that had to be followed. Sergeant McGroarty had helped Daddy with the arrangements and people were praising his compassion and generosity of spirit.

185

'A pillar of strength…way above and beyond the call of duty.'

Bssee, bssee, bssee. My head felt woozy. *Bssee, bssee, bssee.* Why were so many people whispering? *Bssee, bssee, bssee.* The house reverberated with the hissing of whispers from solemn mouths that didn't seem to move. *Bssee, bssee, bssee.* There was a continuous drone and I wanted to tell people that they didn't need to whisper anymore.

The living room looked different and for a few seconds I felt disorientated and thought I was in the wrong house when I walked into it. The coffin was set up as the centre piece but that isn't what threw me. The room had been newly wallpapered and it was clean and fresh and seemed almost cheery. There were new curtains on the window and they were tightly closed for the world must be blacked out for death. A small table in the corner of the room was draped with a spotless white linen cloth and on it stood a golden crucifix and some flickering candles and a holy bible opened with a blue ribbon across the print of one page. There was a picture of the Sacred Heart on the wall. Jesus watched in empathy.

Help me Obi Wan Kanobi you're my only hope…

He had a polished halo around his head and his languid hand pointed to a burst of sunrays coming out of his chest and his sad eyes gazed only on the coffin.

Karen pinched my arm softly. 'Are you okay?' she said.

I nodded indifferent. Nodding and shaking the head seemed to be the designated physical responses.

'Eternal rest grant unto her…,' I said to myself as I went over to the coffin and bowed my head. I was determined to say a prayer.

'…eternal rest…grant now as I lay me down to sleep…I pray if I die before I wake…all the kings horses and all the kings men…humpty dumpty eternal rest in peace…eternal peace…couldn't put Lauren Doherty together again.'

I blessed myself thinking that would encourage something, maybe the words would flow. Prayers were fairly automatic once you had a prompt, but no prayers came. I knew that I had given up on the hope that prayer was supposed to bring, it wasn't the first time that prayer had let me down and it would be a long time before I would ever pray again.

Karen put her arms around me and we rested our heads on each other's shoulders and I could feel the wetness of her tears on my neck. But I couldn't cry and I didn't deserve to cry…why the fuck should I cry…I had no right to feel anything.

Daddy never broke breath to us that entire night. In the room with the coffin he was sitting forward with his elbows resting on his knees, his hands cupping his face. After a few minutes he raised his head and looked us up and down before rising stubbornly from the chair and leaving the room to spend the rest of the time wandering to and fro between the kitchen and the hall and looming in the doorframe and refusing the tea and egg sandwiches that were continuously offered to him.

'Ach, go on now Joseph, a wee drop of tae will keep your strength up!'

He raised his hand to signal his refusal. He avoided our eyes. Sometimes he whispered with the men. Sometimes you thought he was standing behind you but mostly you knew he was biding his time.

I don't know if Elizabeth and Joseph believed that she was in the coffin for they were just told that she was and nobody seemed to know how to explain why. But Marie and Patrick and Neill all knew why she was there but I couldn't look at any of them for they were the lost souls in the limbo of infants, too young to have committed any personal sin but not free from original sin. None of us could ever again look at each other without knowing the evil of our creation and I had let them all down and that there was nothing left in me of the person that I had been.

Death march, media circus

Look at the coffin with golden handles, Isn't it grand boys to be bloody well dead?

Daddy helped carry Lauren's coffin, him and a few of his friends. Johnny the man himself, McCafferty of course was there and Sergeant McGroarty was also a pallbearer, all the fine and strong upstanding men of the community righteously doing their bit in the hour of need. The local stoats of Rathford.

Let's not have a sniffle, Let's have a bloody good cry.

They moved and swayed in time, their arms wrapped firmly around each other united and their taut faces all dutifully bowed,

And always remember the longer you live, the sooner you'll bloody well die!

Father Hannigan had conducted the funeral service, but you knew he was aggrieved to do so. If it hadn't been for Monica's tears, and the chat of the congregants, Lauren might not have been buried on consecrated ground. There was talk about her having to be buried in another parish by a more sympathetic priest.

Father Hannigan was pious and proud of his old school beliefs. He firmly believed that the act of death without God's sanction was an unforgivable wrong and not only against God in heaven but also against his Holy Church on earth. But the predicament was now on his shoulders and Lauren's Last Rites had become his reluctant responsibility. She was part of his flock after all, but you just somehow knew that he felt like he was betraying his conscience, betraying the word of God.

I had noticed Miss Noble talking sternly to him outside the sacristy as we were shuffling into the chapel. She was waving her finger wildly in the air. Father Hannigan had shrunk to the size of a school boy being told off by the headmistress. Miss Noble clenched the collar of her coat with one hand and rested the other firmly on her heart. When she had said her bit, she strutted away.

During the sermon Father Hannigan's unusual monotone delivery confirmed my suspicions...he had not one iota of belief that she would be forgiven for what she had done. There was no pointing in the air dramatically, no attempt at passion in his voice and he wasn't his usual animated self.

So Father Hannigan had to be coerced into doing the deed and he deliberately kept his eulogy short. A few words muttered about how she would be missed by her devoted family and how she had been a dutiful wife and mother, in the way God made a woman to be.

Father Hannigan wasn't alone in his reticence for the air was one of general reluctance as we shuffled from the chapel and proceeded to the graveyard and Lauren's coffin was lowered firmly into the ground while Father Hannigan sprinkled the holy water.

We therefore commit her body to the ground; earth to earth, ashes to ashes, dust to dust; in the sure and certain hope...

And then he paused...and then he coughed and then he closed his eyes and uttered the last words as if he was a criminal, who had no choice but to admit his crime...

... of the Resurrection to eternal life.

It was still frosty and the grave reminded me of the flowerbed. It made me think that the gravediggers must have had a hard station cutting deep down into the frozen earth. There are so many flowers and it is strange to see so many flowers in winter and they look stunned and cold and didn't look like they would live very long.

Monica cried heartily and had to be held up by her sister the entire time. My granda Joe had finally managed to leave the house, but there was no emotion in his face. He might as well have been a stone cold statue standing among the other stone cold statues in the graveyard.

Pearl wore a large black hat with an impenetrable net veil that concealed her face. You knew it was her underneath it and her hiding her shame as she sniffed occasionally, for effect. Nobody really seemed to know how they should feel so they did their best to appear sombre.

Ellen stood back from the graveside. She seemed far away. She was pale and tired and strong and broken. I didn't know how to console her and she nodded reassuringly to me any time I caught her gaze.

Mad Annie zigzagged unnoticed among the mourners. She quietly skipped through to the graveside and gave Karen's and my hand a simultaneous squeeze as she hissed to gain our attention and whispered,

'Now remember what I said girls…don't be on your own, Annie hears things, Annie wouldn't lie to you girls.'

But I just looked at her dazed. I wasn't sure what she meant. Then she was gone again, gone before anyone told her to clear off.

A couple of newspaper journalists had shown up for Lauren's funeral. Two local papers and one national, their cameras had flashed sporadically as the body was being carried to the graveyard. I made sure I hid my face. Lauren had surprisingly made front-page headlines in the local newspapers and The Sunday Globe.

YOUNG MOTHER OF SEVEN SLAYS HERSELF
BODY FOUND HANGING IN LOCAL WOOD BY
SIXTEEN YEAR OLD DISTRAUGHT DAUGHTER
TOWN LOCKED IN COMMUNITY GRIEF

It's an ill wind that doesn't bring the geek and freak media circus.

There was talk of Monica having a whole middle page article devoted to her version of events in one of the popular Sundays.

TRAGIC MOTHER'S BATTLE OVER DAUGHTER'S
SANITY

So with the newspaper attention, plus the influx of people from the surrounding areas that wanted to offer their support and sympathy, the events had triggered a herd mentality among the local community and you could see that they wanted to keep the stampede going. There was also the added bonus that it was good for business.

After the funeral a reception had been organised, in the Drummond Arms, by Doreen and Don. They felt it was only right. We still had a room there and the entire hotel was booked out and it seemed to have become the designated hub of events.

Doreen looked a bit embarrassed when she saw us arrive back from the graveyard. She was flustered when she told us about the arrangements but Karen and myself and Ellen agreed that we would only join the post funeral gathering for a few minutes.

We walked among the troupe with our heads lowered while voices droned around us. School friends were talking about their memories of her during those early days and admitting that they hadn't seen *height nor hair* of her in years. As to be expected, there were stories and rumours and innuendos being passed from person to person until they would become an acceptable version of events in the small town collective memory.

Some people said that Lauren had been having an affair and she was afraid that Daddy would find out. Others were saying that the madness was in the family anyway and Aunty Rita's name had been bandied about a few times. All I knew for sure was that Lauren was gone and that would never be any different, that was the one thing that couldn't be undone. No story could ever bring her back.

My hands were aching from people coming up to me and squeezing them.

'I'm wile sorry for your loss, wile sorry for your troubles, sorry, sorry, sorry, god bless you, sorry.'

I had to pull the sleeves of my cardigan down over my hands and put them behind my back…I couldn't bear anybody touching me…but hand gestures seemed a necessary part of the ritual so instead people rubbed the tops of my arms.

Marie, Elizabeth, Patrick, Joseph and Neill hadn't been allowed to come back to the Hotel. They were deliberately being kept away and had been quickly whisked back to Monica's.

'It's no place for wains, there's too much talk,' Monica had said.

'They don't need to hear the talk. They're far too young and innocent to understand.'

Some people said that Monica had gone home to get ready for her interview. The reporter in question wanted her to tell her story while the events were still clear and the story was newsworthy.

We were offered food but couldn't eat anything and after we had passed ourselves we quickly decided to make our excuses and leave.

'Aye…we are just going for a wee lie down…sure we're exhausted…it's been a tough few days indeed!'

The three of us were trying to be as quiet and discreet as we possibly could and we just managed to get to the door of the reception room when Doreen met us at the pass. She was flustered and unusually dishevelled and she was very sorry but she had had a complaint from one of the guests.

There are no shortages of moments in your life when people confront you with their prejudices and sometimes they are nothing more than throwaway comments that you couldn't give a rat's arse about. Then there are those times when comments can really annoy you and you relive them in your head until you have rewritten an ending where you get the last word. But occasionally there are moments when people speak and you know that they are nothing more than a full-time bigot and in fact you should be left dumbstruck. We were about to be confronted with one of those moments.

Doreen began to mumble, she seemed a bit embarrassed and there was a group of women, *hubble bubble toil and trouble* huddled near us watching her intently.

Doreen explained that it wasn't necessarily her point of view but that Mrs Peterson had asked her to say something.

'What has Mrs Peterson got to do with us? I don't know the woman at all.' Ellen said incredulously.

But I did, I knew who Mrs Peterson was. She was the walking chemist. Mrs Peterson had more tablets, pills and

192

concoctions in her on any given day than could be found in any chemist shop in the world. She had been at deaths door for years and was a sickly being, according to her on-going self-diagnosis; for she nurtured her illness well and made sure that everyone was updated regularly.

'When I got to the hospital, my kidney was actually hanging out.'

That was the kind of thing you would overhear her saying.

'Well you see.' Doreen said and then she stopped.

'Oh dear God...I'm sorry girls...this whole thing is wrong.'

Then she turned and shook her head at Mrs Peterson.

Mrs Peterson mustered up her best self-righteous look and walked haughtily up to us and for a woman on death's doorstep her step was pretty firm.

Doreen looked defiantly at Mrs Peterson. 'I think these people have been through enough and there is no need to add to their grief. I think it would be better if you left well enough alone.'

We stood there in disbelief. We had no idea why Doreen was asking Mrs Peterson to be quiet. No idea at all.

Mrs Peterson looked Ellen square in the eye.

'Please,' Doreen said, as she tried to step in-between them but it was of no use. Mrs Peterson was going to have her say.

'I feel it would be more appropriate if you used the toilet in your room.'

'*Why*?' Ellen asked visibly taken aback. Doreen didn't speak. Mrs Peterson sniffed the air like an aul workhorse that realises the weather is about to change.

'Why?' Ellen asked again. This time her voice was steady, she was going to make her explain.

'Well you see, I don't keep well and the papers warn us about the things that the likes of you...'

'It's not my thinking Ellen, not for one minute, ladies let's just...' Doreen interjected.

But Mrs Peterson interrupted and left Doreen visibly mortified. There would be no stopping her.

'I don't think it's safe to use the toilets after you, without them having been disinfected, given the kind of things I could catch from your kind.'

Nnnn, nnnn, nnnn. Mrs Peterson ran the sentence out of her mouth as if she was confidently sewing a straight line on an aul Treadle sewing machine. I had been reared in a small town and I had heard some stupid shit over the years, but this topped everything.

'Are you serious?' Ellen said, raising her eyebrows in disbelief.

'Are you really serious?' This time Ellen raised her voice and all eyes in the room were once again feeding on us. People held their drinks in mid-air and the silence was audible.

'Oh fuck off, you pack of fucking homophobic witches.' Ellen's tone was one of complete and utter disgust.

'Fucking stuck in the dark ages!'

'Well it's true,' Mrs Peterson interjected.

People sipped their drinks and replaced them onto the surface tension, ready for the next instalment.

'It's a fact that people like you…with the stuff you get up to…'

We didn't listen to the rest of what Mrs Peterson was saying. We walked away. Karen and I each took Ellen by the hand. We wanted to show her our support and I could feel my Daddy's eyes cutting into our defiant backs.

'Look', Doreen said following us out of the room, 'I'm so sorry about that…look Ellen I know you're not like the way people say you are...'

We didn't listen to the rest of what Doreen had to say, we walked in shock and disbelief back to our room.

I was disgusted at the way Ellen had been treated but Ellen said that they weren't worth getting ourselves all worked up over because she didn't expect any better from a crowd of backward redneck hillbillies.

'Ignorant people use their haughty judgements to mask their narrow-mindedness.'

Although Ellen said she could have expressed herself more eloquently in the reception room for her outburst and choice of words is exactly the reaction they would have wanted but on the bright side there would be plenty of prayers offered for the salvation of her soul.

To you do we send up our sighs, mourning and weeping in this valley of tears.

The world had certainly fallen apart and we didn't know how to make it begin again. But the one thing we did know for sure and that was that we couldn't stay at the hotel forever but we just didn't know how to leave. And then the quiet again, the eerie quiet, and it filled the hotel room until it seemed like we didn't know how to speak. Three days passed and the gates of hell were once again thrust opened and no-one could ever have anticipated what they were about to unleash.

Book X

Rathford, County Donegal
Present Day

For him the bell tolls

I had jumped the wall of the graveyard and was happily hiding in some flowering gorse bushes that smelt like the coconut cream biscuits and I was sneakily duking over the fortification like Black Paddy or Mad Annie would have done. I certainly didn't feel stupid or mad or like a crazy loon halfwit cretin and I was enjoying getting a clear and unequivocal view into the way my life would have been if I had stayed in good old Rathford town. I would have been branded the mad aul woman of the roads, hiding in hedges, stealing chickens and generally avoiding people like they were the flea ridden rodent carriers of the bubonic plague.

I had realised that I couldn't bear the thought of standing among the mourners. Their grief was by no means mine and I was relieved that I had finally felt the conviction of that conclusion and it wouldn't have mattered if Martin or Ellen were standing right by my side. Enough was more than enough and I had paid the penance piper and I didn't belong here and I never had and the thought gave me a sense of release.

Free at last, free at last, Thank God Almighty, I'm free at last.

I felt a kind of devilish peace and I was smiling and I knew that if anyone had caught a glimpse of me the parish exorcist would definitely have been called in.

'Aye, she's thonder in the corner of the field, see how she can't stand on the hallowed ground…hiding herself behind the wall…she has a mad grimace on her face and the divil is definitely in her.'

High above the church St Conall's bell began to clang…ding dong ding dong…announcing that the ceremony was over…ding dong ding dong… I watched silently as the mourners emerged into view…ding dong ding dong…the coffin was raised sombre in the air…ding dong ding dong…floating as if it had acquired invisible

197

wings and was slowly levitating instinctively towards its final resting place.

People intuitively circled the hole in the ground as the priest took up his commanding officer position at the fore. He began to chant and his voice held the same vibrational tone like the death knell as it resounded into the sky.

'Let us commend Joseph Michael Doherty to the mercy of God,' his voice traversed like a wave sending the sincerity of his plea to the heavens.

'Muck to muck, clabber to clabber, filth to filth, and manure to the great big festering dung heap in the bowels of hell.'

Then the priest held his breath so all felt the finality of the full stop after the word 'Amen'. The ceremony had reached its close.

People shuffled, mumbled, nodded and hands were shook. I was as quiet and still and as a timid little water shrew for I knew there was no such thing as sudden movements at a funeral. All gestures must be despondent and sombre and people would eventually and dolefully disperse. I remained in position until I could no longer hear the solemn tones. I had waited years to travel from the heart of bonny Scotland to hide behind a wall. I felt no need to chastise myself, as far as I was concerned all had passed swimmingly and no better sound to hear than that of the shovels slicing into the rich clay and the splattering of the dirt being scattered onto the coffin with hollow sounds.

Annie was nowhere to be seen, but I didn't think she would be too far away. I had a bit of an inkling that I wasn't the only watcher.

Put forth to watch, unschooled, alone, 'twixt hostile earth and sky; The mottled lizard neath the stone, is wiser here than I…

So that was that…it was all over...done and dusted, finale, finito, fin, kaput, dead and buried!

I began to count up to three hundred in my head…just to let a few minutes pass without feeling unproductive and when I reached my target I was ready to make a move. Tis always better to let the dust settle for a few minutes and I didn't want to bump into any stragglers.

I crawled silently along the outside of the wall maintaining my shrew-like demeanour until I again managed to locate the stile. I stood up and stretched. A choir greeted me.

Morning has broken, like the first morning.

The world was alive and rejoicing.

Blackbird has spoken, like the first bird.

It sure was good to be among the living.

Praise for the singing, praise for the morning. Praise for the springing fresh from the word!

The gravediggers had buried themselves in their work and were well on their way with filling in the hole.

'Did you know Joseph?' One of them looked up and spoke inquiringly as he rested his chin on the shaft handle of the shovel as I moved forward to loom over the coffin. Of course I ignored him and his snooping question.

'A fine man, the life and soul, had his hardships as well.' He rubbed his nose with his sleeve and examined the deposit of mucus.

Again I didn't answer. My eyes had been draw to the tackiness of a wreath in the shape of a violin. The repugnance helped me fill my mouth with saliva. I rolled it between my teeth and tongue until I was confident that I had accumulated an adequate amount of spit.

'AAAccchkkkktowt.' I spat vehemently on top of the coffin.

'Hey misses,' one of them said, 'what the hell…there's no need for that carry on!'

I turned and walked away. They were still calling after me but I had no reason to listen or turn around.

I headed back towards my car. It was parked in the front of the chapel. I wanted to sit in it for awhile and gather my thoughts. McGroarty was on my mind and I had to make a decision about what I would do next.

I circled round the chapel once again and uttered a fond goodbye to the holy statues. I felt we had grown familiar again during our short reacquaintance.

'Clear.' A voice shouted in my head, I felt as if the pads of a defibrillator had been placed over my chest and an electrical charge had been sent to my heart.

'Clear.' I need a second shock to bring me back. McGroarty and a few of the men were talking with the priest as I walked into the car park. I didn't stop walking while I quickly retrieved the car key from my handbag.

Clunk-click…the central locking responded to the remote control key and I kept my head down and my body hunched over as I stayed focused on getting into the safety of the car but I needn't have worried because nobody acknowledged me, nobody turned around to look and there was no Mexican standoff, no Ennio Morricone soundtrack.

I shut the car door and settled myself into the driver's seat. I watched the assembly disinterestedly for a few seconds and then I knew that Adele Doherty was alive and well for I had a sudden urge to switch on the ignition, revvvvve up the engine and smash them all down like bowling pins.

'Strike!'

Book XI

Rathford, County Donegal
1987

Hounds of hell

My heart is as black as the blackness of the sloe, or as the black coal that is on the smith's forge; or as the sole of a shoe left in white halls; it was you that put that darkness over my life. You have taken the east from me; you have taken the west from me; you have taken what is before me and what is behind me; you have taken the moon, you have taken the sun from me; and my fear is great that you have taken God from me!

It was about three thirty in the morning, Karen and myself were sound as a pound asleep in one of the single beds in the Drummond Arms. The room must have been cold for we had snuggled close together. Ellen was asleep in the other bed. Until that night we seemed to have slept in shifts, almost like there was always one of us on guard duty but for some reason that night all three of us had fallen into a deep sleep and probably for no reason other than sheer exhaustion. But looking back now I don't think it would have made a damn bit of difference, even if we had all been awake.

The door was suddenly and violently kicked open. All three of us awoke with a start, bolting upright, our hearts racing. Daddy bounded into the room and Sergeant McGroarty followed. The air was choked with the smell of alcohol. It filled the room like a fog. I knew instinctively what the smell meant.

'Get up girls, get up!' my Daddy yelled. 'Get your things…for you're coming home with me, your Mammy's dead and there's not much we can do about that now…you're coming home with me tonight.'

'I'm not going…I'm not going anywhere with you.' I screamed and Karen was objecting also.

Daddy grabbed both of us forcefully at the same time. He had caught us by an arm each and dragged us out of bed, jolting and bumping us together. I felt like my arm was going to come out of its socket!

'You can't be staying here with the likes of that one. I know what she wants! Do you not know why she likes girls?'

Ellen was on her feet, but Sergeant McGroarty reached for her and twisted both her arms behind her back.

'You have no rights over those girls…let them go with their Daddy.' Sergeant McGroarty held Ellen firm as she struggled to fight off his grip.

'I know what that dyke wants to do to my girls, I'll fucking cut your hands off if you have laid a finger on them, do you hear me you fucking freak.' Daddy was roaring at Ellen.

'Cut my hands off you piece of shit.' Ellen shouted back at him. 'Cut my hands off if that makes you feel better about what you done. You need someone to blame Joseph. You need this to be somebody else's fault, you murdering piece of shit.' Ellen winced in pain from the force that McGroarty applied as he pushed her hands further up her back.

Daddy was enraged by what Ellen had said and seemed to lose interest in us momentarily. We began to struggle and wriggle fiercely. We fought with every twinge of physical strength that we could muster to get away from his hold. Ellen's shouting was helping our attempt to escape and his grip wasn't as firm. Daddy stared violently at Ellen.

'What the fuck did you call me you dyke piece of shit!'

'I called you a murdering piece of shit…you fucking bastard cunt of a man.'

Ellen spat at him.

The globule landed on his shoe and he looked down at it…then slowly and fiercely he raised his gaze again and at the same time I felt his grip loosen. I yanked myself sideways and somehow managed to slip free. I pulled Karen and she slipped free also. We had fallen onto our hands and knees and we scurried frightened, crawling towards the bathroom. We clambered inside and pushed the door firmly with our shoulders and frantically managed to get the bolt across. Our hands were shaking violently and our eyes filled

203

with tears. I was leaning against the door. Then I noticed a kitchen chair and I lifted it and lodged its back firmly under the door handle. I had seen someone do that in a film one time.

Daddy was kicking the door. The frame shuddered and I felt like the entire wall was going to come down. We hunkered down on the floor trying to make ourselves invisible.

Then we heard Ellen shout at him again.

'You fucked Lauren up in the head, you piece of shit, for God sake give those girls a chance, you have enough blood on your hands! Leave them be.'

Then Ellen was struggling to speak and sometimes her words were muffled and sometimes she managed to free her mouth from McGroarty's grip and we could hear her curse them and she never gave up.

'You're a fucking bully Joseph…fuck you and your pig friends….!'

And then the attempts at kicking the door in got weaker and weaker and then the kicking stopped. But the noise and the shouting didn't stop.

We heard a loud slap and it stung our faces and we put up our hands to protect ourselves and Ellen continued to shout.

'Did that make you feel better, did that remind you what it was like when you beat Lauren to a pulp.'

Karen and myself cowered in the bathroom and we could hear Ellen's voice and we could hear furniture being moved and we could hear muffled screams and we could hear Daddy and McGroarty cheering and goading each other.

'This is what a real man does, this is what you have been asking for all these years…'

The things Daddy was saying lasted for a long time. I knew what they were doing to Ellen and I knew if I went out that McGroarty would hurt me. I couldn't let him hurt me again and I couldn't stop what they were doing to Ellen.

'Karen,' I cried. 'Karen what can we do? I know how they are hurting her…Karen make them stop hurting her.'

Karen didn't move and she kept her face buried in her hands. Then we could hear sobbing, and I knew it was Ellen. I hadn't heard her cry before but I knew it was her. Then, the silence again. The terrible silence and I couldn't find any words to keep the silence from my head.

The room began reeling and my eardrums vibrated. Suddenly there was no sound. Then a snap like a branch from a tree and the world faded to black.

Desecrated shrine

'Open the door girls…it's alright, you can come out. Open the door.' A woman spoke softly to us from the other room. I couldn't open my eyes and someone was shaking my shoulder.

'Adele, are you okay? Adele.'

I didn't want to get closer to the voices. I wanted to stay in the dark. Then the voice beside me was no longer soft and it started to rise in panic.

'Adele wake up. Adele…it's me, Karen. Please wake up Adele. Please.'

The name was familiar and the voice was familiar, and all I knew was that if I opened my eyes, I would have to look at something I didn't want to see.

'You need to come out,' the woman spoke again. 'It's alright, they've gone and they won't be back. It's alright to come out.' This time I recognised her voice. It was Doreen.

Then Ellen spoke.

'Open the door girls. It's only me and Doreen in the room…you're safe to come out.'

I could hear shuffling and I knew Karen was reluctantly removing the chair from under the handle.

'Please don't open the door,' I said. 'Please don't open the door.' But it was too late and I opened my eyes and crawled forward.

The door was badly damaged and the wood had splintered at the base and it sagged wearily on the hinges.

I raise my head a bit and saw that the bedroom was a mess and most of the furniture was broken and the wardrobe had fallen forward. The blankets had been pulled of the beds and were tossed and strewn around the room.

'I couldn't stop them.' Doreen said. 'They were all drinking downstairs in the bar and everyone was in good spirits. And then somebody said something about the girls being up here with you and the kind of things that you would be doing to them. I couldn't stop them…he just flew into a rage…your Daddy…he just flew into a rage…but I know what they done to you Ellen, Jesus, Mary and sweet Saint Joseph. It's terrible and in my hotel, Jesus, Mary and Joseph I know what they done…they're a pack of animals. A pack of bloody animals.'

Doreen had run out of things to say but her mouth was still making sounds but they were incoherent.

I couldn't raise my head. I didn't want to look at Ellen. I felt like I would break into smithereens if I looked at her.

Then Karen suddenly fell to her knees and knelt in front of Ellen and she bowed her head like a sad figurine kneeling at a desecrated shrine. Ellen was wrapped in a blanket and her eyes were swollen from crying. They must have ripped her night clothes off because they were lying torn on the floor. Karen cuddled into her.

'I don't know what to do.' Karen said sorrowfully as her body began to shake and tremble.

'What have they done to you?' she whimpered.

I stayed under the doorframe of the bathroom and still couldn't move forward.

'I'm sorry.' I began to say. 'I'm sorry, why did they do it…how could they do it.'

'Ellen, I'm so sorry, I should have warned you. I…we …Lauren.' But I couldn't say it.

'Ssshhh.' Ellen said. 'We need to get packed…we need to leave tonight.'

Getaway

I had been given an instruction and if I concentrated on it then my mind would keep working.

'Gather your things together as quickly as possible, girls.'

Ellen said we needed to leave so I knew that leaving must be the right thing to do. I couldn't think about why or how. I knew that if they came back they would kill her. They would kill Ellen, get rid of her body and throw it into some isolated bog-hole that no-one could ever find.

I needed to stay close to Ellen and at the same time I was trying to find the few things that I had from among the debris, but I didn't give a shit about our belongings. I just wanted to be away from this room…so that Ellen could be safe.

Doreen sat with us while Ellen showered. We waited outside the broken door. It took her awhile, well at least it felt like a long time and I thought I could hear her cry again through the hissing and spraying of the water.

'I want to kill him.' I said to Karen. 'I want to kill them.'

Karen stayed quiet. She didn't help me gather up our clothes. She just sat on the edge of the bed with her head down and I didn't know what to say to her. I didn't know why she hadn't spoken, but when Ellen finally came into the room again, I was stunned when I discovered why.

'I can't leave them.' Karen said to Ellen. 'I can't go with you and leave them behind.'

I suddenly knew who she was talking about and the revelation left me dumbstruck for I hadn't given them a second thought. Just like Lauren, I hadn't thought about the others.

'I can't leave!' Karen spoke again. 'What about Marie and Patrick and Elizabeth and Joseph and Neill?' The despair in her voice was pitiful and she choked over each name.

'They're still with their granny.' Doreen answered. 'They're still in Monica's house.'

'I'm sorry Karen but we have to go tonight, we need to get away, then we can work something out, I promise we won't forget them...but we have to go now.' Ellen's words held no consolation for Karen.

'I can't,' she said. 'I can't go without them!'

'Ellen's right,' Doreen said. 'You have to go tonight, I heard the way they were talking in the bar. They are a law unto themselves.'

'There's no bus until the morning.' I said deflated.

'I have the hire car.' Ellen said.

'They'll be watching that.' Doreen answered.

Oh Jesus was there no way out of this god-forsaken place? I wanted to get down on my hands and knees again. I wanted the blackness to swallow me.

'But if we got as far as the boat,' Ellen said. 'I could get someone to meet us. I have a friend who could pick us up.'

'Take my car,' Doreen suddenly said. 'Take my car, it's parked out in the back and you can go out the fire escape and nobody will notice it missing. I'll think of something to keep them off the scent for awhile. Take my car Ellen and drive to Larne or Belfast or wherever. Get on the next boat you can, and don't look back, don't look back for the love of God.'

'But what about the others!' Karen stood up and asserted herself and stomped her foot like the determined child that she was.

'I need to get you two away safe.' Ellen said. 'There are things we can do then, but I need to get you two away first.'

'I won't go without them.' Karen said again. 'I'm not going anywhere with anyone without them!' Karen had rooted herself determined to the spot.

'Do you not care about them Adele, do you not care about them even a little bit.' She shouted.

'I do care. I do care. I do care...' I fell onto my knees and began to hit my temples with my fists. 'I do care.' If I hit my head hard enough the blackness would come back... 'I do...I do...'

Ellen knelt beside me and gently pried my hands down and held them together.

'We're leaving Adele, we're going right this very minute, you're going to be okay.' She whispered sadly as she turned to look at Karen.

'Isn't that right Karen…we're leaving right this very minute.'

I couldn't see Karen's face but I knew she didn't want to change her mind.

'What if he hurts them?' And her voice was still choked. 'What if him and Sergeant McGroarty does…' But Karen stopped and looked sorrowfully at Ellen. 'I know Mammy only wanted Adele to go and not the rest of us!'

'Oh Jesus Karen,' I shouted at her. 'Lauren didn't know anything, she didn't even know who I was…she didn't remember anything…she didn't know what she was saying or doing.'

'But you did, you knew what she was doing, you knew!' Karen faced me and she was steadfast and what could I say to her? She was speaking the truth. I did know what Lauren was doing, I had helped her and I could never change that.

'I can't do this, I can't do this anymore, please make it stop.' And I started to rock again and…

'Karen please,' Ellen said. 'We have to go.'

'Come on girls…we need to get you away…' Doreen tried to intervene but it was a half-hearted attempt.

'I'm not going…I'm not leaving them.' Karen said again.

Journey to a new land

Karen cried heart-sore for the first hour of the journey then she sobbed and buried her face in her hands. She couldn't stop crying…not even if she had tried and you knew that her sobs came from a place of desperate hurt and pain, the kind of hurt and pain that only the sound of helpless tears could express.

Ellen quietly told us that it was going to be about a three-hour drive but the roads were quiet and we would make good time. There was no moon to watch us and the car headlights were our only guide as we moved forward into the night.

Every now and then Karen would whimper the same thing, 'I'm not going…I can't leave them.'

Ellen shifted uncomfortably in her seat and I stared straight ahead at the road as the front of the car propelled us forward and greedily consumed the white line road markings.

We had to stop at a checkpoint at the Derry-Donegal border. Two soldiers with vigilant eyes stepped out from a booth and peered suspiciously into the car. They didn't look much older than I was and I felt embarrassed.

'Where are you going?' one of them said to Ellen.

'Scotland.' Ellen answered.

'And where are you coming from?'

'Rathford,' Ellen replied.

'Where's that?' the soldier asked.

'It's a small town, just on the outskirts of Letterkennedy.'

'And the purpose of you visit?' The soldier nodded as he seemed to grasp the co-ordinates.

'We are returning home after a short break with family, we're getting the late boat from Larne.'

'Okay, on you go,' he said, 'and have a safe journey, it's a still night, the sea shouldn't be too choppy.'

Karen had pretended she was asleep. The soldier smiled in at me in the passenger seat as he waved us forward. He was the first person that we had met in days that didn't know who we were.

Ellen drove for another few hours and I wanted us to never stop driving into the night. If we kept moving no-one could ever catch up with us. But once again there were street lights and Ellen stopped the car and a man's head stuck out from a small booth and asked her a few questions. Ellen's answers must have been appropriate because a barrier lifted up and we drove into the dock. A huge metal boat was moored and the back was opened and cars and Lorries were coming out of its hull.

Ellen parked outside a kiosk and told us to stay where we were for a few minutes. She said she was going inside to get our tickets and organise somewhere for Doreen to collect the car keys.

We waited for a short while until Ellen returned. The Lorry drivers called jovially to one another from their cabs. They seemed familiar with the place. The smell of diesel was thick and occasionally you got a strong waft of the sea breeze while gulls daringly squawked and flew in and out between the vehicles.

We walked up a metal ramp and it vibrated beneath our footfall. You could see water beneath it and it looked like melted tar. The boat rocked gently and then the engine growled. I was trying my best not to feel afraid or nauseous as the boat turned and navigated out of the dock.

My last look at Ireland would not be captured in some heartfelt emigrant's song. It was with great relief that I watched it disappear from the dirty window of a P&O ferry. Neither would I be crooning an Irish Lullaby. I clung desperately to the hand railing and outside the wind went whining past and my fear of the water made my stomach churn and my eardrums pulse. The lights of Larne Harbour soon faded one by one into the cold dark past until the only thing I could see was the white foam of the Irish Sea slopping against the side of the boat.

Transfiguration

Back in Rathford, in that dark house beside the humpback bridge and past the beech tree that had been cut down and the flowerbed made out of a tractor wheel and the rusting barrel that catches the rain water and in through the scullery door and past the kitchen and into the narrow hallway and through to the sitting room with the ashes dying in the grate, somewhere in the shadows of that room there is a set of hardback encyclopaedias. They are made up of fifteen separate volumes and are collectively called *Childcraft*. Each book specialises in some specific area and they have names like *Make and Do* or *Stories and Fables*. Book number one in the series is called *Poems and Rhymes* and when I opened that book the world became a sacred place and I was drawn to one particular poem for I couldn't believe that someone could write something that asked the very same questions that I asked the world every waking hour of my life.

Will there really be a morning? Is there such a thing as day? Could I see it from the mountains, If I were as tall as they? – Has it feet like water lilies? Has it feathers like a bird? Does it come from some country, Of which I've never heard? – Oh, some scholar! Oh some sailor! Oh some wise Men from the skies! Please to tell a little pilgrim, where the place called morning lies!

The poem was on page eighty of the book and was alongside a picture of a young girl dreamily sitting on top of a cliff and her yellow hair is windswept. The most beautiful clear blue sea crawls beneath her and a young boy plays on the sand with a dog. The girl wears a blue dress and holds a pink hat with a green ribbon in her hand and the flowers around her on the hillside are the same shades of pink and green. The beauty of the poem always made me hope that maybe one day it would be possible to find the place called morning…a sunrise Shangri-la El Dorado.

I walked off the boat that morning shivering with the cold and exhaustion and anticipation and relief. The docks seemed more

213

open and less claustrophobic than the dock at Larne and the sky was a dome of grey clouds but the breeze felt lighter.

Ellen's friend, Martin, who over time would become my closest confidant, was waiting to meet and greet us in Cairnryan.

'More refugees!' He applauded as he spoke in a feminine voice and presented us each with a single white gladiola.

'Well, let's get you some food, clothes and shelter, youse look like youse have been twice round the block and through the mill backwards. Us castaways must stick together.'

He opened the back door of his car and bowed gently as myself and Karen climbed willingly into the back seat, we couldn't help but smile back at him. Martin closed the door and then went round to the front of the car to where Ellen stood. He took her in his arms and held her in a loving embrace. She began to tremble and hid her face in her hands but Martin tenderly removed her hands and softly kissed away the tears from her cheeks and her eyes. He was speaking soothingly to her but we couldn't overhear what he was saying and you knew he would have held her like that forever if that's what she needed him to do. I was amazed more than embarrassed. I had never in my life seen anyone display such a natural expression of love. Somehow you knew he understood how to reach the depths of hurt with genuine unconditional affection.

Ellen eventually took a step backward but they still held onto each other by both hands and they looked into each other's eyes and smiled only for each other and they were the only two people in the whole world.

'Right, let's hit the highroad.' Martin said as he turned on the car ignition.

'And I think a bit of music wouldn't go amiss…I havnay got a copy of Donald wheres your troosers but this is the next best thing!'

Martin played a Sister Sledge tape in the car as we drove up the Scottish coastline towards Glasgow. He pointed out Paddy's Milestone and other landmarks to break the silence and he jovially sang along to the music but especially to *We are family, I got all my sisters and me!* He even managed to make Karen smile with that one and a couple of hours passed quickly and we reached the largest city in Scotland.

Book XII

Glasgow
1990

Caledonia's been everything I ever had

It took us a brave while to settle down and adjust to our new life in Glasgow. Ellen owned a two-bedroom cottage flat in Kings Park. The houses were compacted together in little white washed blocks of four. Two flats down stairs and two above. Ellen's flat was half way up Curtis Avenue and the road twisted around like the neck of a goose and the houses stood like perfect little sandcastles, evenly poised and positioned all the way up to the top. I liked the symmetry. It gave me a feeling of things being where they belonged.

To begin with we didn't leave the house. Every little noise set us on edge, the traffic passing outside, the noise of people constantly walking on the footpath outside the house, the glare of the streetlights at night. I liked the streetlights. Karen said she missed the darkness.

Ellen had a lot of friends who made us feel welcome but I liked Martin most of all. Martin and I just seemed to connect instantly and I felt like I had known him since the start of time. He only had to walk into a room and I had the broadest smile on my face. Every drop of life was precious and beautiful when you were in his company.

Martin had grown up in Westport in county Mayo. I loved the curves of his accent. Every single syllable was worthy of pronunciation. He didn't sound at all like McGroarty.

Martin was honest and sweet and cursed anybody to hell that had a bad word to say about anyone that he cared about. He told us that he had to leave Ireland because of the 'shock- horror-cardiac-arrest' reaction that his family and local community had when he announced that he was queer as folk and their idea of queer was completely different to his.

'Aye' tis a queeeeer morning that's in it and I had a queeeeer fish for breakfast.'

So because Martin's family couldn't cope with the story of Adam and Eve becoming the story of Adam and Evan they had decided to match-make him, for they thought that marrying him off would stop all the speculation, quieten the gossips and give a semblance of normality to their outspoken son. Martin said that he initially went along with the scheme because he enjoyed the wedding planning side of things but had a change of heart when he realised that it wasn't a laughing matter. He regularly recounted the story with hilarity for it was often requested at dinner parties and get-togethers.

'Now as you can imagine, a date had been set for the *big day* and I was ordered to go and attend this pre-marital course, with this poor agricultural lass who hadn't a clue, god love her. She was no more attractive to me than the man in the moon. Well, actually the man in the moon might be worth checking out! Mental note! Anyhow, when the priest began to explain the part in the ceremony where he would ask did anybody have any objections to the union…I suddenly had a moment of clarity. I told him that as a screaming queen I felt it my Christian duty, to let him know in advance, that there may be one or two objections to my entering the institution of Holy Matrimony. The priest was at first bemused and thought I was just taking a hand out of him but when I began to name names…a few fine upstanding men in the community that I'd had had several *les liaisons dangereuses* with…his expression changed to one of sacrosanct disgust and well he refused to marry us. He told me I was the most despicable person he had ever met…*abomination* I recall was his word of choice…so he gave us our marching orders from the parochial house and told my parents about what I had said. They were mortified, of course, cut clean to the bone. So they gave me a few pounds and told me to bugger off. They said it would be best if I stayed away for a decade or two.'

Martin worked for a theatre company as a make-up artist and had developed a good reputation. I spent a lot of time with him and he taught me how to fix my hair and make the most of myself. Now I know I am no oil painting, but I'm not one of the aul 'Bingo Bus' Biddy's either.

'If you have it, flaunt it,' Martin would say, 'and sure if you can't hide it, decorate it!'

Martin pampered me a bit I suppose and I felt safe in his company. It was a whole new theatrical dimension for me and a far cry from the Rathford pantomime. I would go along to the different theatres that he worked for and was able to watch the performances from the wings but to be honest I mostly stared at the audience. I was fascinated by how people's faces changed during the course of the show and altered in the different lights or with the action. I would attribute beliefs and opinions and attitudes to them. I became aware that no-one is ever a passive watcher and the true meaning of any story is in the way people react or try not to react.

I loved my outing with Martin and grew to completely trust him and I confided in him more than Ellen. Although part of me knew that he fed back some of the information between us. He cushioned things that I couldn't have told Ellen, things that were too painful for us to talk about. There was no hidden agenda with Martin, no personal gain and above all no ulterior motives.

Karen's never stopped being heartbroken about having left the others behind and I know she resented me for settling down and not wanting to talk about our lives in Rathford. After the first few weeks passed Ellen told Karen that it would be best to see if we could legally do anything. The solicitor we went to was very pragmatic about our situation. She advised us to lie low if we wanted to stay in Glasgow. Daddy could lawfully bring us home, but she said that the best she could do was drag her heels if necessary, delay things until enough time passed and he was no longer legally responsible for us.

But nobody looked for us. No official letters arrived, no police called at the door, nothing and three months just slipped past.

Karen couldn't adjust, she missed the others terribly. Maybe I was more selfish, I don't know. Wild horses couldn't have dragged me back to that place.

I tried to tell Karen that Lauren just seemed to pick a point in her life when she felt able to make decisions, and she had blanked out so many things. I knew I was like Lauren that way. If I couldn't cope with something, then I just blanked it out.

I knew Karen wasn't consoled and she became more and more withdrawn and sometimes days passed and we didn't even speak to each other. I would have given her that last morning with Lauren if I could have…if that is what she really wanted but I knew there was nobody or nothing to take it away from me. Karen's fight with her rage and sadness made her even more determined not to forsake the others.

Glasgow belongs to me

Three months quickly dissolved into three years and I turned nineteen. My life had changed in ways that I never knew it could. Myself and Karen had attended a nearby secondary school and Ellen had encouraged us to get a good education and she made sure we worked to the best of our ability.

'A good education is not to be sniffed at.' Ellen would say suspiciously when we tried to negotiate sick days off school.

The school was so big and everyone there seemed so grown up and confident. Most of the young women wore make-up and had wildly permed hair that was dyed in all sorts of luminous colours. There was a constant bustle about the place and incessant excited chatter about music and films and who was going out with who and stuff that happily meant absolutely nothing at all.

'Dinny say that, right, a didnay kiss him, he's an arse wipe, I wouldnay touch him way a barge pole!'

Everything was a million miles away from Rathford. Life just didn't seem so intense, so scrutinised and nobody really gave you a second glance, not even if you painted your face white and had a million body piercings.

Karen did well at school, she didn't mix the best and was insular and focused entirely on her work. She always got good marks in her examines. I did okay and although I didn't fail at any subject I wasn't an 'A' student or anything that might indicate the genius tendencies that I know I possess. I suppose school taught me how to be average and being average suited me fine. That way I didn't stand out. There was no pressure to do any better or worse for that matter.

Those first few years in Glasgow were a time when me and Karen should have been growing closer together but the unspeakable separated us and only served to push us further and further apart.

I would often catch her staring at me and I knew exactly what she was thinking and I know now that if I hadn't acted all crazy that night in the hotel then Karen would never have got into that car with us. It was my fault that she had felt coerced into leaving.

I was just so relieved to be away from everyone and all that had happened and most of the time I don't have to remember. Then some word or gesture or look slips me back. I come downstairs and she has come back to the kitchen and she is crying and she tells me that I have to help her. Then I am in the forest with her and I climb the tree and I fix the rope because she doesn't have the strength to do it. I burn my hands on the rope and I close my palms tight so no-one will see and I turn my back to her. I turn my back as she puts the noose around her neck and I want to look at her and I hear her voice thanking me. She thanks me for helping her, 'one more thing,' she says, 'just one more thing', and then everything becomes foggy again and I am looking for her and I can't find her in the fog. Sergeant McGroarty is there and Daddy is there and Monica and Pearl and the newspapermen are there, and they won't let me go into the woods to take her down from the tree.

Karen didn't have that trauma and she didn't have the pain of McGroarty that day in the woods either and because I couldn't tell her she was never going to understand. That is another price I paid for silence.

In summer of 1990, we all got up on the morning of Karen's eighteenth birthday and she was standing in the kitchen with her bags packed. Karen told us that she was returning to Rathford. She had waited until the very day that she was no longer legally considered a minor and said that she was going back. When she was ready to leave again Daddy wouldn't be able to stop her and six long weeks passed and she came back to Glasgow to tell us that Daddy had remarried.

Karen filled us in on all the details saying that Daddy had wed within six months of Lauren's death and that Monica had kept the others until that time but she had been nagging him to take them back. They were too much work for somebody her age. She couldn't afford to feed and clothe wains on a state pension. Granda Joe was enjoying having the boys around and he was teaching them about carpentry and stuff but he never had the ability to stand up to Monica and in the end she always got her way. The attention Monica had got initially had worn thin and her martyrdom wasn't being catered to and why should she look after somebody else's children if there was nothing in it for her?

So one day, out of the blue, Daddy appeared with a woman from Fanad. They had met at some dance and he had proposed to her that very night. I hated the thought of him using some sad story about Lauren to make her feel sorry for him.

Daddy moved his new woman into our house and moved the others back in with them. They randomly spent their time moving back and forth between Daddy's and Monica's. Karen had to meet with them in secret for when Daddy saw her on the main street in Rathford he walked straight up to her and spat on her. He never spoke a word, he just spat on her and walked on. But Daddy couldn't intimidate Karen and she stayed in the hotel with Doreen, although things weren't too good there either. When Sergeant McGroarty found out that Doreen had helped us, he kept having her fined for opening the bar after hours until eventually she lost her drinks licence.

Don had taken to the drink, in all the years before he had been a t-totaler but after that night he took to the drink with ferocity. Doreen said he could do whatever the hell he wanted. He had been the one who would not let her go up to the room that night and she could never forgive him for that. He had held her downstairs and told her it was none of their business.

Don now slept in a separate room in the hotel and she said she only allowed him to stay because she felt sorry for him and he was pathetic. Doreen said that Don wasn't without blame and there was no man in him.

Doreen was well able to hold her head high and didn't care what anybody said or thought. She never regretted what she had done. She said it wasn't much and anyhow she wished she hadn't been so high and mighty.

The hotel was a mess and Karen helped Doreen to clean the place up a bit.

Father Hannigan had been moved to another parish. A mother of one of the altar boys had put in a complaint about him to the Bishop. She had walked into the sacristy one day to collect her son from Altar practice and found Father Hannigan with him sitting on his lap. There was going to be an investigation. A couple of others witnesses had come forward and Miss Noble had made a statement to the Gardaí and then she too was gone, like ourselves, in the dark of night. There were stories about her now working in the fields of Athenry for some other priest.

Monica had come to see Karen in the Drummond Arms and told her that she had been warned not to be looking for us. Monica cried and said she had prayed and she was sorry but that Karen looked grand and she was glad we had been well looked after.

'I hope that Ellen one didn't do anything she shouldn't have to you.' But Karen had told her not to be stupid and that she wanted to see the others.

Pearl wouldn't come to see Karen for she was getting on the best with Daddy's new wife for she could drive a car and her and Pearl toured about the place together, going on shopping outings and to the bingo and wakes and Céilís.

Eventually Monica managed to bring the others to see Karen. She had taken pictures of them and Jesus I couldn't stop from welling up every time I looked at them. They were amazing, it made them real again and I wished they weren't in the fog. I wished I could spit the lump from my throat and tell them why I had run away. They had grown up so much.

But the most shocking thing of all was the fact that Karen was going back. She said that Daddy deserved to look at her every day and be reminded of Lauren. She would be close to the others, which is what she always wanted. Doreen had said she could stay

224

with her in the hotel and maybe they would open it up again. There was a bit of a property boom about to hit the county. People had started to clear land that had lain fallow for years. Doreen and Karen could run the hotel as a B&B if they didn't get a drinks licence, sure it might be better that way anyhow. They could pick their clientele and not have to serve the halfwits that were running about the place.

There was talk of Sergeant McGroarty retiring early to build houses on land that he had bought and there was a possibility that a new Sergeant would be in the town and you never know, he might even be okay.

I couldn't tell Karen not to go. I knew that even if I had told her about what McGroarty had done to me that it still wouldn't have stopped her. I had taken her away and she didn't want to leave in the first place. I had to let her go back.

I couldn't even wish that I wanted to go back with her. There was no part of me that could go back, not even for the sake of my brothers and sisters. The thought of it just made the fog settle thicker over me and I couldn't move. I was paralysed again and then the pressure and the scrutiny of so many eyes, abrading each day like course sand paper on skin. I was a coward who couldn't return to the scene of the crime.

Ellen was worried about Karen going back and she knew better than most what they were capable of but she hugged Karen and told her that she always had a home here with us, no matter what. She said Karen could come back any time and bring the others if they would come. The door was always opened and besides she had a key. It was like something Roberta would have said.

Ellen couldn't go back either. She never really spoke to us about the pain of that night, about what they done to her. And I never told anybody about what McGroarty done to me, not even Martin. I couldn't speak about it because Ellen believed that she had protected us and I couldn't tell her that it wasn't true.

So Karen went back alone to Rathford, back to Doreen and her Drummond Arms, back to the precarious hotel standing sentry over the river.

Ellen and I left Karen to the bus and I hoped that she would be all right. She seemed to be determined and was stronger than I could ever imagine being. Karen my sibling, Karen the only person that meant blood relation, Karen the sister that I could never be, Karen the good and the gracious and the kind and the sacrifice and the brave. Karen walking back into the lair of evil. Karen and all I could never tell her. Karen the compassionate. Karen the crusader. Karen who would try to give recompense for what should never have happened to any human being in any place or time.

I waved her off mournfully and watched as the bus slowly got sucked into the traffic. I knew I would never see her again and although we would keep in touch, over the years the contact became minimal, and in the end I lost her as well.

Karen stayed with Doreen and they became a great business team. Eventually Karen would marry and have children of her own, like most of my siblings and as the years disappeared Ellen and myself would receive an occasional wedding invitation but we would always come up with some reason as to why we couldn't go. Life just carried on without us, just like ours passed without them.

I belong to Glasgow. Dear old Glasgow town, well what's the matter with Glasgow, for it's going 'roon and 'roon…

I map the streets of Glasgow in my head. I walk up Hope Street and onto Sauchiehall Street and down Buchanan Street and try to image that I am leaving my essence on them and my ghost will never have to return to Rathford. I know what that place means to me and how it grew me and that it turned me into the shadow that I am and ultimately the only thing that it ever taught me was how to hate myself. The mirror of home is all the pain that makes you feel that you are not worth or deserving of any love in your life.

Ellen too had to escape and when she returned what happened to her was the most malign attempt at the annihilation of someone's soul. Ellen, more than most, deserves some sort of reprisal. I know Karen didn't deserve to go through what she did either and my brothers and sisters ought not to have been left behind…left in a world where you are slowly and methodically broken and downtrodden and utterly dumped upon… abandoned children littering the fields of other people's lives, trying to pick up the pieces of half-truths or falsehoods.

I think sometimes Ellen worries about me. Worries that I would do the same thing that Lauren did. But she doesn't have to because I can survive trudging along and I have been working in a shoe shop for years, in a shopping centre in the heart of Glasgow. I remind myself daily that I fit in and that I belong to a world where life just passes you by because when you have seen the world as it really is, you can't be in it anymore. Everything you do becomes pretence and that is the best place to be because nothing can ever hurt you again. So you just copy the way other people get on with things and that way you can choose what the story is. Choose what is real or not and you don't have to feel the pain or disappointment or rejection or all the terrible things that we pretend don't exist inside of us.

And most of the time I'm just like everyone else that puts in a week's work, waiting on my wages so I can buy new clothes or pay a bill. Mundane things like that make me feel strangely safe. But I know I'm not like everyone else for some days I see her on Argyll Street and I follow her, 'one more thing,' she always says, 'just one more thing,' as she disappears into the crowd.

And of course I know it's not her, it's just someone who looks like she might have looked if she wasn't hanging frozen in the woods and that's when I think Karen is lucky because even though she decided to go back, at least she is there, trying her best to live among the living. Trying to move on and repair some of the damage that was done while I am unable to help her, unable to be truthful with myself or with the rest of the world. Well at least not until Karen contacted me to say that Daddy had finally bit the dust.

Book XII

Rathford, County Donegal
Present Day

The End

Everyone considered him the coward of the county. He never stood one single time to prove the county wrong...

I didn't leave the church car park until everyone had dispersed. As usual, there would be a post funeral do on somewhere and everyone would be raising a drink to the good health of Daddy's memory. Reminiscences would be exchanged and glasses refilled.

His mamma named him Tommy, the folks just called him yellow, but something always told me, they were reading Tommy wrong...

I knew I had a boat to catch and that Martin would be feeling anxious if I was running late but I had a new story in my head and there was nothing that could put off my notion.

Twenty years of crawlin' was bottled up inside her. She wasn't holdin' nothing back; she let em have it all, When Adele left the barroom not a Rathford boy was standin', and she said, 'this one's for Lauren, as she watched McGroarty fall...

I sat in the car for awhile. I needed to formulate my plan quickly and I could see no reason to delay putting it into effect, once the details were straight and adequately visualised.

I would go out to 'oul Jonny the man himself's place first. There was a piece of equipment I needed to procure before I went to the forest to get everything ready. It would save me time later on. The roads would be quiet and the first part of my plan would be easily constituted.

I wasn't surprised by how emotionless I felt. I was just doing what I had to do, what should have been done a long time ago.

I caught my reflection in the car window as I locked it up, having pulled in out of sight at the edge of the forest. It made me laugh and I stared amazed at how authentic my disguise actually was. I could have fooled myself for I looked like one of the aul biddies that went to the bingo, wearing me over sized coat and a headscarf that was tied tightly under my chin and my national health glasses and all.

'Oh Jesus Martin, I'm sorry, I know the disguise was only so that I could go to the funeral. But opportunity has knocked and fuck it I have to answer. I might never be in this neck of the woods again.'

The forest was much the same as it had been almost thirty years earlier. It had been replanted in parts, but that didn't disorientate me. Where I needed to go was easy to find. I had seen it in my mind's eye every day. I found the old stone house easily. There were no ghosts waiting on me, no poems or songs in my head, the place felt serene and ready.

Some things don't change, well it's mostly people that don't change, for habits and routines set early in our lives are patterns that we feel comfortable with. It's hard to break the habits of a lifetime and nobody knows that better than me.

It was Thursday night and I knew the men would hold their card game in honour of Daddy. Well at least that's how they would justify going ahead with it.

'Awe sure lads, it's the way Joseph would have wanted it…'tis no disrespect to his name!'

I would have to wait awhile, 'till the *Poitín* kicked in and they would be well leggered anyway from drinking in the pub.

Leggered */leg girrrr id/* n. This is a made up generic word used to confuse foreigners when trying to figure out the last time an Irish man or woman has actually paid for a round of drinks. In reality the word has no discernable meaning whatsoever. Any attempts to discover the meaning, if there is one, would result in a thickening Irish brogue, or in worst case scenario, rapid Gaelic. The Irish use this word whenever they think that you are too close to understanding what they are saying. 'ye've bin bog surfin den Errigal an youse are all leggered now ye loon ye' which roughly translates without the word *leggered* in it as: you **halfwit cretin handlin.**

It would be the wee small hours before they were all asleep. Sure what was wrong with that. It would save me anaesthetising the bastard, using that chloroform stuff, doused on a dove white linen handkerchief that they use in films. I wanted it to look like it had been his idea. I mean I was prepared to do time, but if it could be avoided, then I was going to avoid it as best I could. They had got away with terrible things and sure why couldn't I give it a go myself.

'Play the game boys…play the game!'

Whack for me daddy-o, whack for me daddy-o, there's whiskey in the jar-o

I waited in the darkness outside 'aul Jonny's the man himself's' house! The craic was good and the conversation flowed with stories about Daddy. Now I have to say that was tough, a couple of times I had to stop myself from bursting in and telling them that they were all talking a load of bullshit crap. I could see myself with an AK47. Rat-a-tat-tat spraying the place with bullets and replacing the magazine with military precision, until the entire shack collapsed with the onslaught. But sure a drive by shooting wasn't really Donegal style revenge.

I would let them have their fun and it wouldn't be long until it would be all over. I felt like one of the musicians of Bremen, looking in the window at the robbers and their ill-gotten gains.

I was waltzing with my darling…there was a child named Bernadette…don't it make my brown eyes blue…trailer for sale or rent…

I was desperately trying to find a theme song to go with the occasion but in my excitement nothing seemed to suffice and the hours ticked passed and their frivolity slowly started to ease back and soon there were only a couple of voices and then there was only some shuffling and then there was the silence and it was the first time I had waited on silence.

231

Gentle at first and then deeply the snoring came and it resounded like a dirge and rose to fill the air, deep unconscious snoring, like the music at a funeral procession.

I strutted to the barn to get the homemade wheelbarrow. I had seen it earlier on my reconnoiter visit. I have to say it was a fine piece of construction, an excellent specimen of invention and ingenuity. A car tyre was used for the wheel and the barrow's wooden frame was elongated and box-like, like a coffin. The handles were long and it balanced well when you pushed it along.

I entered the house, focusing on what I was there to do and I began to escort Sergeant McGroarty off the premises, well wheel him really. I just tipped him out of the chair he was lying in. He slumped comfortably into the wheelbarrow, shimming round like a slippery fish, until his limbs eventually hung comfortable over the edges.

McGroarty groaned for a few seconds while he settled into his new accommodation. He was far, far away in the land of nod, and in his sprawled comatosed state his huge rib cage looked like an inviting trampoline…

The wonderful thing about tiggers, Is tiggers are wonderful things! Their tops are made out of rubber, Their bottoms are made out of springs! They're bouncy, trouncy, flouncy, pouncy, Fun, fun, fun, fun, fun! But the most wonderful thing about tiggers is…I'm the only one!

But no time for bouncing about…there was plenty to be getting on with!

I had to heave with all my strength to lift the wheel barrow and push forward with force to get the momentum of the wheel going. McGroarty's body was heavy and the creaking of the wheel every time it performed a revolution encouraged me and gave me a rhythm to move to. The wheelbarrow wobbled a few times but I managed to maintain its equilibrium and the muscles on my arms ached and felt like they were going to pop out through the skin but it wasn't long before I had reached the car and tipped him into the back seat.

'Come on now, there's a good boy…in you go…sleaze bag Fuck Head McGroarty…bastard sick fuck cunt!'

I pushed him all the way into the back seat with my foot, ramming him slightly and again he groaned but he was so loaded with the drink I had no fear about him waking. I closed the door carefully but I wasn't too worried about the noise levels because I knew that the explosion caused by Nelson's Pillar being blown up wouldn't have roused that fucker out of his inebriated coma!

I drove discreetly again to the edge of the forest, I didn't need to switch on the car headlights…I mean I could have travelled that route blindfolded.

I opened the car door and began to drag McGroarty out of it and into the woods, but he felt heavier now and it was getting harder for me to keep pulling him. I dragged him a bit more, then rested, then dragged him another bit. I began to wish that I had had room in the car to bring the bloody wheelbarrow with me. My limbs ached and I knew it wouldn't be long until morning and I needed to be a million miles away before that happened.

The dawn chorus was rehearsing and I was starting to feel annoyed and then I swear on my mother's life that it suddenly sounded as if they were singing *Nearer My God to Thee*. I began to hum timidly along with them.

I was getting tired and McGroarty's feet were leaving tracks in the ground and I didn't want it to look like he had been dragged and I would have to go back over the tracks and clear them somehow.

I was starting to feel upset, maybe I could just kick him to death, kick his fucking head in. That would make me feel good, but I knew I had to stick to the plan. It was always when people diverted from *the plan* that things went wrong.

I had a sudden urge to scream, there were words in my throat that had been there for too many years and I felt that if I could

233

release them I would somehow feel renewed. But the defeat that I was starting to feel engulfed me in a sudden swoop and I sat down and buried my head in my hands. The birds were in tip-top form singing away uninterrupted and I sat there like the little girl on the ditch and I didn't want to be the same stupid wee girl of all those years ago, so near and yet so *Nearer My God to thee…Nearer to Thee*…and then I began to pray and it was truly a divine moment. The *our Father*, the *Hail Mary* and *The Glory Be* suddenly fell from my lips and tasted as fresh as a newly sprung mountain spring. I was elated! The prayers were on a loop and nothing could make them stop…*Thy kingdom come, thy will be done on earth as it is in heaven*…I stood up and felt as if I was about to transcend or something.

'Alleluia, amen, praise the lord!'

I was thinking that I could check out 'the born agains' when I got back to Glasgow. And my mind was flowing like the river Jordan and then I knew that I wasn't alone.

I'm not sure at what point she arrived, maybe she had been watching me for awhile. Maybe she had followed me from the town. But I just suddenly knew she was there and I jumped and turned to look at her in the same moment that she softly placed her hand on my shoulder.

'Come on now, Annie will take his feet.' She reassuringly said.

Mad Annie had emerged from the shadows and I was so stunned that I sat down again.

'Get up!' Her voice was firm. 'Annie will take his feet…Annie and Adele don't have much time.'

I got up and done exactly what I was told and we both carried an end of McGroarty's weighted body. It sagged in the middle and sometimes it dragged along the ground. But we were making progress and we stumbled fervently through the forest. Then we began to pray together, mumbling contently like devout pilgrims. We didn't need to talk about anything and we just kept praying with unfaltering devotion. God was finally listening to me and he had sent an angel to help.

We went exactly to the spot where we needed to be and all was still at the ready. My preparations hadn't been disturbed. The rope that I had procured earlier from aul Jonny's the man himself's barn was waiting and swaying patiently like the clock pendulum.

Annie and myself didn't need to discuss *the plan*, both of us knew roughly what we needed to do. The noose barely went over McGroarty's head snagging on his nose. I dragged on it around his neck until it was tight. Annie tried to lift him with her arms under each knee but was unable. In the end we had to scramble with me pulling the rope looped over a sturdy branch. Annie taking the weight of one side of him. I'd swear in the madness of it his arm raised up once to fight us back. It was as if he had moved punch-drunk with a fist. At last we had him, slumped on his knees while the noose and rope kept him from falling over onto ground. We had a hell of a job getting him onto his feet while pulling the rope until suddenly his boots were an inch or two in the air. Four times we let his feet back onto the clay but with our will and strength got him hoisted up. He looked like the prize catch. I only had to stagger backwards holding the rope at full tension without slipping in the mud. My hands burned on the fibres as I encircled the tree trunk twice before knotting the rope.

The surprising thing for me was that I didn't need to look him in the face. I didn't need to see him choke for breath. I didn't need to see Fuck Head one more time.

We walked away without looking back and Annie smiled craftily at me. We could hear the weight of McGroarty's body making the tree creek as he swung.

'Annie will whoosh the cows out of the upper field and lead them through the forest and make them run riot over the muck.'

Jesus Annie was a clever one. They would cover our tracks.

'Thank you God, thank you God for Mad Annie!'

'Annie misses Adele, Adele was good to Annie, Lauren was good to Annie, Annie misses a lot of good people.'

I gave Annie a warm hug before I got into my car and drove into the first rays of morning and you gotta admit it…even a sunrise in shitville looks pretty!

Printed in Great Britain
by Amazon